The Beiderbecke Tapes

'That's really weird.'

'Did I see your lips move?' asked Jill.

Trevor removed the headphones. 'It's this tape. All the others are jazz. This one's got Beiderbecke written on the outside, but I just started listening to it, and it's men talking.'

'What about?'

'It sounds like . . . the dumping of nuclear waste.'

'Give me those headphones. You mark the rest of the books.' She handed him the nine remaining exercise books, and took the headphones from him.

'You have to sandpaper the shelves as well.'

'How do I work this thing?'

'Press the switch marked switch.'

Trevor settled down with Holden Caulfield and Billy Casper. He occasionally helped Jill with the marking of essays, on the strict understanding that he knew nothing of the subject and would therefore assess every piece of work at the same level: '7 plus – promising'.

Trevor marked the essays. Jill listened to the tape.

'Is this role reversal?' said Trevor.

'Whyebuggerman!' said Jill.

ALAN PLATER

The
Beiderbecke Tapes

A Methuen Paperback

A Methuen Paperback

British Library Cataloguing in Publication Data

Plater, Alan
    The Beiderbecke tapes.
    I. Title
823′.914[F]   PR6066.L3

   ISBN 0-413-60340-7

First published in Great Britain 1986
by Methuen London Ltd
This edition published 1986
by Methuen London Ltd
11 New Fetter Lane, London EC4P 4EE
Copyright © 1986 by Alan Plater

Printed and bound in Great Britain by
Richard Clay (The Chaucer Press) Ltd,
Bungay, Suffolk

For Stephen, Janet and David

The Beiderbecke Tapes

One

It was the best of terms, it was the worst of terms. To be sure, the staff and students at San Quentin High had no fixed opinion about the summer term, except relief when it was over.

It was a time of stress, as fresh-faced young people sat GCE and CSE examinations, jousting with their future on one side of the paper only, knowing the deeds they did that day would determine their individual destinies, perhaps leading upmarket to compulsory redundancy from cinema-management – perhaps downmarket to permanent unemployment in hod-carrying.

It was also a time of stress for the teachers. Those too slow on their feet to dodge the headmaster, Mr Wheeler, found themselves organizing sports days, summer fayres and school trips. Their only consolation was the certainty of rain on the day, and the inevitable drenching of school governors and minor apparatchiks from the Town Hall. That made everybody laugh, apart from the drownees. It rained on most summer days in the outer limits of Leeds, and even when the sun shone the people agreed, cheerfully, that it wouldn't last. The local voters had refined their scepticism to an art form matching Florentine frescos or Gregorian chant; they would not accept a Holy Grail without reading the small print first.

The staffroom at San Quentin enshrined many of the

longer-standing traditions of the educational system: acrimony, petty jealousy, bad debts and stale smoke. The teachers were united only in a distrust of Mr Wheeler, and a resolute opposition to his best-laid schemes, on the basis that most of them were crazy. The headmaster had a dream that his school should go down in the annals – any annals would do – along with names like Eton, Harrow and Rugby. He hated the fact that everybody called the school San Quentin High, and cherished a hope that one day a former student would become Foreign Secretary in a Conservative administration. To date, his most eminent former pupils were a prop forward with Bradford Northern, a Bluebell Girl and a failed bank robber doing a ten-stretch on the Moor.

Mr Carter, time-served history teacher and cynic, loved to observe at least three times a day: 'We are a beacon of learning with a frayed wick.' The first time he said it, some of his colleagues smiled, but nowadays they had generally left the room already. Mr Carter was an accomplished emptier of rooms and, aware of this prowess, had a growing ambition to clear the entire school playing field on sports day by the use of well-worn aphorisms and epigrams, before the end of the third race.

Apart from his obsession with applied boredom, Mr Carter was also fascinated with the behaviour of certain of his colleagues, notably Jill Swinburne and Trevor Chaplin. He would tell them, 'You two are the human condition, writ small.' Jill and Trevor would reply, often in unison, 'Knock it off, smartarse.' In the staffroom of San Quentin High, this was regarded as pretty swift repartee. It was also sincere.

Mr Carter's fascination with the Swinburne/Chaplin relationship was shared by a great many people around the school. They could not understand the powerful, if intermittent, attraction that united these two. In the red corner, Jill Swinburne, English teacher, conservationist, feminist and battler for good causes like blue whales, the majority of trees and ideologically sound toilet rolls; in the grey corner, Trevor Chaplin, woodwork teacher, Geordie-in-exile, jazz freak and ten years Jill's elder. Jill walked about as if expecting a new Jerusalem; Trevor walked about as if retreating from Moscow.

Jill had an additional quality that worried people. Her O-level English students tended to pass their examinations, a transgression not easily forgiven at San Quentin High.

Her relationship with Trevor had begun three years earlier when her marriage broke up. He had offered her a lift in his crumpled yellow van, the lift had become a regular habit and out of the acorn came forth an oak: a mutually supportive, ongoing how's-your-father, as Trevor called it, complete with occasional visits to the Film Theatre to see award-winning movies from Eastern Europe, and less occasional adventures under the duvet, with inhibitions eased by *vin ordinaire* from the beer-off.

The summer term had witnessed a considerable lurch in the Swinburne/Chaplin liaison; whether a lurch forwards, backwards or sideways remained to be seen. Trevor had moved into Jill's house on a permanent basis: a physical and emotional lurch in anybody's language, though Jill suspected they were lurching on the spot.

Trevor's moving in did not imply a deeply felt, long-term commitment, but a recognition that his own house had been demolished. It did not happen without warning. A letter had arrived several months earlier. As they drove to school that morning, they had discussed the implications.

'I'll be homeless, I'll be a refugee, I'll be dispossessed.'

Jill had reassured him: 'Don't worry. We can save your home.'

11

'It's an attic flat. You can't save it on its own, if they demolish the rest of the house. Gravity's against you.'

Under the duvet that night, in the consoling afterglow, Jill had announced her conclusions: 'We won't give in. I'm a time-served conservationist. I know every nook and cranny of the planning regulations. Come to that, I also know every crook and nanny in the Town Hall. We will never surrender.'

'We can't fight them on the beaches. Leeds is too far inland.'

Trevor had insisted on watching the demolition. Jill went with him to make sure he didn't stand too close. A huge iron ball on a formidable chain crashed into the ornate Victorian facade, built in an era when Gladstone was prime minister, Gentleman Jim Corbett was world champion, and the composers, Godwin and Dryden, were writing 'The Miner's Dream of Home'. Within minutes, the house was reduced to a handful of dust, thereby putting it in much the same category as Gladstone, Corbett, Godwin and Dryden.

'I thought you knew about the planning regulations?' Trevor had murmured as the echoes of falling masonry died on the wind of the Wakefield mistral.

'I do. We had no chance.'

Jill's rationale was formidable. If the house had belonged to Trevor, instead of a dubious property company from whom he rented it . . . if the letter of protest had been posted in time . . . if the building had been of historical and architectural importance . . .

Trevor was under no illusions. 'It was a dump. But it was my dump. I'll miss it. My stains on the carpet. My life. My history. My traditions. My achievements.'

'Sentimental fool.'

But as Trevor gazed across the newly created stretch of urban desert, Jill, momentarily touched by his yearning for lost dreams, real or imaginary, had taken his hand, and it is a frighteningly short step from a laying on of hands to an invitation to move in on a permanent basis.

The summer term was a season of mutual discovery. Jill had not lived with anybody since gently but firmly hurling her ex-husband from her life. Trevor had not lived with anybody since leaving his home in downtown Sunderland to go to training college. Habits and affectations, endearing on an overnight assignation, scratched more deeply on a daily basis.

Trevor liked to make faces with his food. Given a salad, he would transform a tomato into a nose, cucumber into a mouth, radishes into eyes, with lettuce as hair and chutney as a jaunty moustache. Red and green peppers, which had rarely touched upon his takeaway bachelor existence, added new dimensions to his creativity, until Jill stopped him.

'*Must* you make faces with your food?'

'My mother used to do it when I was little, when I wouldn't eat. Just got into the habit. It's fun, isn't it?'

'The first time, yes. The twenty-ninth time, less so.'

'I do amazing things with chicken vindaloo.'

'Not here, you don't.'

He also developed a habit of trivial and generally unwanted consultation. One morning, while shaving in the kitchen – the bathroom had no shaver point – he asked Jill: 'You're into the environment, aren't you?'

'Yes.'

'Are the hairs in and around a man's ears of any use? Or should I shave them off?'

'They're your hairs – do as you like with them. But don't drop the bits in the sink.'

'I'll shave the outsides and leave the insides.'

The great test of the new living arrangements arrived on Day Four of Cohabitation, with the arrival of Trevor's record collection, which had been stored, double-locked, in the woodwork room at San Quentin High. Jill was resigned to his obsession with jazz, and even made occasional jokes about it. Reading her *New Statesman* resolutely through side one of the latest LP, she would gently inquire: 'What's this one? Julius Caesar's Pieces of Eight or Jelly Roll Mingus and the Hot Club of Hounslow? And what time does the tune start?'

'Knock it off, cohab.'

She could live with the music, just as he could live with the *New Statesman*. It was the sheer volume of space occupied by the record collection that appalled. It filled dozens of cardboard boxes. Removed from the boxes, it filled every horizontal surface in the living room.

'How many records have you got?'

'Don't know. Never counted. Maybe a thousand. Or two thousand. Not including the tapes.'

'Tapes?'

Trevor reached into yet another cardboard box and produced a cassette by way of evidence.

'Thank you, Trevor, I know what a tape looks like.'

'And the amazing thing is, every one of these records, and every one of these tapes, has a story attached to it. For example . . .'

He picked up a record, more or less at random, and launched into a cheerful reminiscence, eyes shining.

'Dizzy Gillespie's big band at Pasadena, 1948. This brings back memories of getting legless on Chianti and falling off an elephant.'

Jill ignored the story, though she was briefly intrigued by the elephant. She flung out her arms in a despairing gesture of Camille-like proportions.

'You have taken my home and turned it into a garbage dump!'

'That's easily solved.'

14

'How?'

'We'll go down the pub and forget about it.'

This was another dividing line between their contrasting views of the world. To Jill, a problem was a challenge, to be confronted, assessed and vanquished; to Trevor, a problem was something to leave until Thursday.

As often happened, their immediate solution was a compromise. Trevor agreed to make some shelves on which to store the two thousand records; he was, after all, a woodwork teacher with many years' experience, and making shelves was a very modest challenge to his skills, akin to asking Rachmaninov to play two choruses of 'I Did It My Way'. On the other hand, Trevor had no wood about his person, a deficiency that limits even a skilled man in the pursuit of shelf-building.

Hence the Swinburne/Chaplin compromise, agreed and carried on a show of hands. They would go down the pub, but once there, they would discuss shelves, probably in depth.

Breweries have strange ideas about the lives people lead. The area where Jill lived was dominated by the Executive concept. Her house was designed in the Executive Pixie style, as were the houses of her neighbours, few of whom were executives except in the broadest sense. She was aware of an executive plumber, an executive clergyman and an unfrocked bank manager who, in his time, had probably been a genuine executive. She had never done a thorough survey, because the majority of the neighbours did not speak to her; the combination of CND posters in the window and an itinerant Geordie woodwork teacher under her duvet meant she was regarded not quite as a scarlet woman, but certainly as a sprightly shade of pink.

The brewery, given the chance to build a pub to service

the locals who, apparently, saw themselves as lantern-jawed, keen-eyed executives, jet-setting around the world safeguarding Britain's future prosperity, arrived at a totally different conclusion. The brewery decided the locals saw themselves as stout yeomanry, with a taste for quaffing a flagon of nutbrown ale in between hay-making and archery practice. Thus the pub, officially opened ten years earlier by a bit player from *Emmerdale Farm*, was christened the Hay Wain, complete with hunting prints on the walls, ersatz Thomas Bewick woodcuts on the beermats and ploughman's lunches with the choice of two kinds of cheese. The locals, who saw themselves as neither executives nor yeoman, stayed away in their thousands, proving that breweries are not exempt from the ground rule: the road to hell is paved with dud intentions.

It was ten minutes' walk through the park from Jill's house to the Hay Wain, and as they pushed their way through the swing doors into the public bar, they were overwhelmed by emptiness and neglect. There was dust on the cabinet that was believed to contain a dartboard and a hint of green mould on the pool table.

They selected a corner table, near the door. It was necessary to keep the real world within easy reach. Trevor crossed to the bar, hoping to catch the attention of a bucolic landlord or buxom barmaid, as promised by the image-makers. Instead he saw a bell-push on the counter. He pressed it, and somewhere in the province, a bell rang. There followed a long, long silence, so long that Jill calculated that if anybody turned up, it would be Godot. Trevor was on the brink of suggesting a bottle of Frascati from the beer-off when a shambling figure in jeans and Greenpeace tee-shirt appeared. He had the gentle, weary look of a man marooned at Woodstock, assured that the answers were blowing in the wind, even if he didn't know the questions.

16

Trevor had half-turned away from the counter and felt the need to apologize.

'Sorry,' he said, 'didn't realize the bell worked.'

'It's so the consumer can attract the attention of the eager and well-trained staff.'

There was nothing in the barman's attitude to suggest eagerness or training, so Trevor assumed this was a joke, but best ignored in case it was not.

'Any chance of a pint of bitter and a vodka-and-tonic?'

'My pleasure.'

He pulled the pint with an apathy verging on grandeur. It took as long to fill the glass as it had probably taken to ferment the yeast. Trevor felt an urgent need to fill the silence with cheerful saloon bar chat. His best offer was: 'Quiet in here tonight.'

'The first four hours after we open, they're generally quiet. Sundays we get labradors and cravats. Soon as I've done this, I'll start the muzak. Get the ambience going.'

Trevor noticed a tape deck behind the bar, and feared the worst. The brewery's idea of appropriate sounds was likely to be 'Do You Ken John Peel' played by the Massed Bands of the Brigade of Guards.

'Well done,' said Jill, when Trevor arrived at the table some time later, carrying the drinks.

'That man is the most inefficient barman I've ever met in my life. A genuine, twenty-four carat lunkhead.' Trevor drank deeply of his pint. 'And the bitter's lousy.'

'Gnat's piss?' suggested Jill, who had sat through the same conversation each time they went in a pub.

Trevor held up his glass to the light. The beer was yellow, opaque and dense with organisms.

'This horse should be shot.'

'A horse or a gnat. It's got to be one or the other.'

'They blend it,' said Trevor.

'All right,' said Jill, irked by his moaning, 'we'll declare this pub black. We'll report the brewery to the EEC, the UN, the Public Health Inspector, the Church Commissioners, the . . .'

Trevor put his fingers to his lips.

'Shhh.'

All Jill could hear was piped music emerging from a series of loudspeakers, discreetly mounted with six-inch iron brackets at various parts of the room, in the yeoman tradition.

'It's only muzak.'

'No, it isn't, it's real.'

The look on Trevor's face was transformed: no longer the dedicated beer drinker betrayed; the smile was gentle and from the Mona Lisa stable, the smile of one who has suddenly encountered the Pacific Ocean, or a Greek urn, or the first cuckoo in spring. Jill recognized the symptoms.

'It's jazz, isn't it?'

'Not just jazz. It's Bix.'

The filigree sounds of Bix Beiderbecke's cornet danced around the empty bar. Beiderbecke, the first great white jazz musician, was one of Trevor's heroes. He had given the lecture many times, to Jill and to anybody else who would listen – how Beiderbecke, born in Davenport, Iowa in 1903, had drunk himself to death at the age of twenty-eight, but in his short career had lit up the night sky with the fragile delicacy of his playing. Jill had heard it all before and now she heard it all again. She even joined in.

'I know about Bix, thank you very much. His playing sounded like bullets shot from a bell.'

Trevor was surprised. 'I didn't realize you listened to me when I talked.'

Though she had decided not to admit it, Jill quite enjoyed Beiderbecke's music. It reached out from an era when people played tunes, pianos had lids and musical instruments in general could function without emergency generators and a truckload of electrical engineers. Jill had a soft spot for innocence, though she feared it would never catch on.

Trevor's innocence was clearly rampant. 'I have never in my life heard real music in a pub. Usually it's plastic music. Raining at the cricket music. BBC2 test card music.' He stood up.

'Where are you going?'

'To investigate this matter further.'

Jill watched Trevor as he crossed to the bar. She knew better than to stand in the way of his obsession with jazz. A year ago his pursuit of a set of cut-price Beiderbecke LPs had led them into a reluctant investigation of local variants on the black economy. A senior police officer had ended up assisting his own police force with its inquiries. Local councillors had found themselves caught with their hands in several democratic tills. A Member of Parliament had trembled briefly and still twitched on cold days. The link between these crumbling empires and Trevor's pursuit of Bix was complicated and tenuous, and he and Jill had given up trying to work it out.

By comparison, this brief encounter with the lost music of the 1920s seemed harmless enough.

Trevor rang the bell on the counter and summoned the ageing hippy.

'Same again?'

'No. Yes. If you like. It's really the music I wanted to talk about. You're a Beiderbecke fan?'

'Yes. Only recently. Used to be into Dylan and Hendrix and the Mothers, you know? Then I saw this television series and it had this like Beiderbecke music, and I thought wow, you know, like wow?'

'You always play jazz tapes in the pub?'

The barman shook his head.

'Sundays the labradors and the cravats complain. So we have sing-a-long-a-crap. But the rest of the time, when there's nobody here . . .'

He waved an arm vaguely in the direction of the empty space round about, indicating that the rest of the time was most of the time. Jill, lonely across the echoing vaults of the saloon bar, wandered over to the counter.

'Any chance of the same again?' she asked.

'Every chance,' said the barman. 'We are fully trained to serve the consumer, as I explained to your husband. Husband?' He realized he was taking relationships for granted.

'Probationary cohab,' explained Jill.

This perplexed both Trevor and the barman, but they decided it was probably none of their business. The beer, when it arrived, seemed brighter and sharper than its predecessor.

'Will you have a drink with us?' Trevor asked.

'No, thank you. I don't accept tips, even in kind. It offends the dignity of the servant. I might steal the odd quid from the brewers but that's more in the nature of a revolutionary act. A blow against the capitalist conspiracy. Would you like some tapes?'

The sudden shift from global ideologies to localized hi-fi took Trevor by surprise.

'Tapes?'

'You like the music. I'll make you some tapes. Write your name and address on there.'

He handed Trevor a beer mat bearing a pseudo-woodcut of what looked like a ferret at bay. Trevor wrote his name, then, the phrase 'probationary cohab' still clattering around the back of his head, added the address of the school. The barman looked at it.

'You teach at San Quentin High?'

'Yes. Both of us.'

'You've done well to survive with your souls intact.'

Trevor and Jill stayed in the Hay Wain until closing time. They unlocked the cabinet and discovered a virgin dartboard which they duly violated. They chipped the mould from the pool table. They remained the only customers throughout the evening and when it was meet and right so to do, they joined together with their friendly barman, shouting in chorus: 'Last orders please!'

It was a much better evening than they had expected and at no time did Trevor Chaplin and Jill Swinburne discuss shelves.

The atmosphere in Trevor's crumpled yellow van was pleasantly benign as he drove Jill to school the next morning. They agreed about everything. The night before had been good fun and neither of them had hangovers. The barman was a sweet and kindly man, albeit weird. They peered through the murk of the windscreen and agreed the weather was lousy. They agreed, totally without rancour, that the living room was a mess and the sooner Trevor put up some shelves, the better. But the greatest measure of agreement was about the glory of the night before and the extreme weirdness of the barman.

Weirdness was at hand when they arrived at San Quentin High. Mr Carter was looking down from the staffroom window, as was his wont. He always said he liked to keep his voyeurism in good trim. The weirdness factor lay in the fact that he was smiling.

'Look at that,' said Trevor, 'Mr Carter is smiling. He could even be laughing.'

'Mr Carter's never laughed in his life.'

Trevor tried to remember examples of Carter hilarity. It was difficult.

'I've seen him smirk. And snigger.'

'There's probably a perfectly abnormal explanation,' said Jill, as they pushed open the main door of the school, being careful not to tread in the broken glass.

Mr Carter was still laughing when they arrived in the staffroom. Jill demanded an immediate explanation.

'Why are you laughing? I know. You ran over a nun on the way here.'

'No,' said Mr Carter, shaking his head, so that the bi-focals perched on the end of his nose quivered, 'though I have to confess that hitting a nun remains one of my subsidiary ambitions. I am laughing at our headmaster.'

He led them through the early morning cheap cigarette smoke of the staffroom to the notice board. On it was pinned an announcement that this year, Mr Wheeler in person was planning to lead the school trip in the summer holidays. The party would spend six days and nights in Holland and volunteers were sought from members of staff to share in the adventure.

'Volunteers,' laughed Mr Carter, 'that's what provoked the hysteria. The idea of any of *us*, volunteering.'

Trevor and Jill had to agree that the notion of volunteering to go to Holland in the company of the headmaster was lunacy of a very high order. This was clearly the consensus view, because in the space headed 'Sign here' there were only two contributions from the staff: a large exclamation mark inscribed with a thick, sincere felt tip, and a footnote: 'Bring your own clogs.'

'Is it free?' asked Trevor.

'Of course it isn't free!' said Mr Carter. 'That's the trouble. You pay your own expenses. The man's a fool. Bribery might work. Or intimidation. But he's appealing to our sense of duty. It's sheer madness.'

'The kids won't want to go anyway,' said Trevor, 'apart

from Three B. They might fancy pushing him into the North Sea.'

It occurred to the three teachers that there was probably a similar invitation on the students' notice board, and it would be interesting to compare responses. They set off to check. Though the notice board in question was on the same floor as the staffroom, the journey involved going down a flight of stairs, along a corridor, across a small quadrangle, through a door, being careful to avoid the broken glass, and up another flight of stairs. The eccentric planning of San Quentin High had never been satisfactorily explained, except that the irresistible purity of the architect's vision had run smack into some immoveable Ministry regulations, with surrealistic consequences. Some students worked through an entire school career, up to and including sixth form, without ever finding the right room.

Mr Carter knew the infallible route to the students' notice board: 'Mr Wheeler put the notices up himself. Therefore all we have to do is follow his silvery trail.'

The holiday notice was crammed into a tiny space between a poster advertising a punk rock concert and an out-of-date leaflet about a carol service. Trevor pointed at the notice: 'There you are, see? School trip. Not a signature in sight. Mr Wheeler's going to be on his own.'

'Nonsense,' said Mr Carter, 'I can see two signatures there already.'

'Read them,' said Jill.

'You know I can't read a damn thing with these new bifocals. You read them.'

Jill read the names aloud, for the benefit of the myopic Mr Carter: 'Francis of Assissi and Sergeant Bilko.'

'Not in my class,' said Mr Carter.

The three of them turned away from the notice board, satisfied that the staff and students of San Quentin High remained united in their policy of full-blooded apathy towards the daydreams of Mr Wheeler.

Mr Carter resumed his contented gurgles: 'It must be some sort of record. A school trip with only one tripper. Never mind. Perhaps a kind Dutchman will give Mr Wheeler a dyke to plug. Haircut!'

The final remark was hurled at a passing fourth former.

'That's a girl,' said Trevor.

'The bi-focals, Mr Chaplin, the bi-focals.'

The three of them went their separate ways, towards remedial woodwork, O-level English and A-level History respectively, though, as usually happened in these situations, Mr Carter went in the wrong direction.

Whenever the headmaster was in pursuit of a vision, the members of his staff made it their business to present a moving target. Mr Wheeler, his academic gown flowing in the architecturally designed draughts that were a hallmark of the school's design concept, haunted the corridors like a thirsty vampire with the scent of a McDonald's in his flared nostrils. Like most paid-up vampires, he preferred his victims solitary. He was intimidated by crowds, whether composed of teachers, students or a combination of each, and there was common sense in this attitude. Issues within the school were rarely resolved on the Socratic principle; dialectically speaking, Rocky Marciano ruled, K.O.

As Trevor, Jill and Mr Carter moaned their way through lunch in the school dining hall, they knew they were safe. Collectively they could outmanoeuvre the headmaster by a blend of low cunning and high pretence, tempered with good old-fashioned lies. Individually, they were vulnerable, most of all Trevor; innocence is an effective protection against many threats, but it does not impress vampires.

Trevor Chaplin chose a route from the dining hall to the woodwork room via the cycle sheds, into the escape exit of the gymnasium – latterly renamed the sports hall, following an edict from the Director of Education – across the middle of a frantic basketball match, through the boys' changing rooms, past the boiler house, up a fire escape, and finally, breathless and undetected, into the woodwork room.

Mr Wheeler was waiting for him, part-concealed behind a palisade of old standard lamps. The students no longer made standard lamps. Because of cuts in expenditure, all new woodwork had to be manufactured from recycled old woodwork. Any kid with ambitions beyond a ruler or a teapot-stand had to bring his own tree.

'Mr Chaplin!' announced the headmaster.

'Yes,' said Trevor, calculating that a denial was tantamount to a guilty plea.

'I'd like a word with you.'

'I'm spending the whole of the summer holidays in Sunderland. My mother's been ill, it's her legs, the doctor says it's psychosomatic but I think she imagines most of it . . .'

Mr Wheeler broke into Trevor's babbling: 'I am not here to discuss Sunderland, or your mother!' He stepped from behind the palisade, into the clearing. 'I was solicited during the lunch break.'

'That's really disgusting.'

'By an exceedingly scruffy man.'

'That's even worse.'

They stared at each other, bleakly. Their conversations invariably drifted into areas where even the cross-purposes had cross-purposes.

'He gave me these.' Mr Wheeler handed Trevor six tape cassettes, tied round with an elastic band. 'He said they were for you.'

Trevor understood immediately. The exceedingly scruffy

solicitor was the barman from the Hay Wain and these were the promised jazz tapes.

'Thanks. I was expecting these.'

'I do not like an exceedingly scruffy man hanging round the school premises, Mr Chaplin. He wore jeans and a shirt advertising green peas.'

'Greenpeace,' said Trevor.

'And I couldn't decide whether he had a beard or not.'

'Yes, I noticed that. Sort of a three-day growth. George Best used to have one. I think you clip it with nail scissors.'

Trevor was now using his favourite tactic with Mr Wheeler. It consisted of throwing free-form irrelevancies together in a bewildering sequence. He had absorbed the technique listening to ultra-modern jazz musicians, where even he had difficulty in hearing the tune.

'What is this man's name, Mr Chaplin?' asked the headmaster, trying to keep the conversation on his chosen theme.

'No idea. He works in my local pub. Protects the dignity of the servant. Hates the labradors and cravats on Sundays.'

'I shall speak to you later, when you're more settled.'

Mr Wheeler crossed to the door, stumbling over a part-dismantled coffee table that predated the standard lamps, before turning with his exit line. He had a fondness for exit lines.

'And he left a message for you, Mr Chaplin.'

'Great. I like messages.'

'He asked me to say to you . . . stay cool, man.'

'I'll do my best, Mr Wheeler.'

That evening, Jill and Trevor disagreed about how he should spend his time. He wanted to listen to the tapes. He calculated they represented nine hours of jazz, and the names scribbled on the containers made him drool, like a red setter on a hot day: Beiderbecke, Parker, Ellington, Lady Day, Dizzy, Prez . . .

'Nine hours of that. Imagine!'

'I can,' said Jill. She had done some calculations of her own. 'I see around me two thousand records that you brought with you. I calculate it would take you eighty-three days and nights to listen to that lot. Almost three months!'

'Whyebuggerman!'

Trevor let out the ancient Geordie cry of delight, pride and awe. Jill was not awed.

'I would like you to use your considerable skills as a worker in wood, and make a shelf, so that we don't have three months of music on the floor.'

'It might need two shelves.'

They reached a compromise. Trevor would spend the evening building shelves, but he would be allowed to listen to his new tapes through headphones while doing so. In this way, he would not disturb Jill, who had to mark thirty-three essays comparing and contrasting the central characters in *Kes* and *Catcher in the Rye*.

By ten o'clock, twenty-four of the kids had concluded that Holden Caulfield and Billy Casper both had a raw deal, and come to that, things were no better around San Quentin High. Jill was delighted with their conclusion. She was also delighted to see two new shelves on the living room wall, so impeccably constructed that nobody would ever know they were made of reconstituted coffee tables. Trevor had worked blissfully, lulled by soft zephyrs from his headphones. He smiled at her as he fed another cassette into the machine. It had the magic word 'Beiderbecke' written on the box. He started to sandpaper the leading edge of the top shelf, waiting for the bullets from the bell, the beguiling music while he worked, the wailing cornet of a haunted man.

27

That is not what he heard. He put down his sandpaper. He frowned.

'That's really weird.'

'Did I see your lips move?' asked Jill.

Trevor removed the headphones.

'It's this tape. All the others are jazz. This one's got Beiderbecke written on the outside, but I just started listening to it, and it's men talking.'

'What about?'

'It sounds like . . . the dumping of nuclear waste.'

'Give me those headphones. You mark the rest of the books.'

She handed him the nine remaining exercise books, and took the headphones from him.

'You have to sandpaper the shelves as well.'

'How do I work this thing?'

'Press the switch marked switch.'

Trevor settled down with Holden Caulfield and Billy Casper. He occasionally helped Jill with the marking of essays, on the strict understanding that he knew nothing of the subject and would therefore assess every piece of work at the same level: '7 plus – promising.'

Trevor marked the essays. Jill listened to the tape.

'Is this role reversal?' said Trevor.

'Whyebuggerman!' said Jill.

Two

Breakfast is the litmus paper of cohabitation. Trevor was at first amused, then irritated by the fact that Jill's newspaper did not carry the sport on the back page, but buried somewhere near the middle. His suggestion that they should take a decent earthy tabloid with the football results boldly displayed where they belonged, complete with banner headlines about managers being over the moon or sick as parrots, was greeted with the response: there is no such thing as a decent tabloid. Trevor did not press the point. The staffroom was always awash with tabloids, most of which fell open at page three.

Food was another potential minefield. An occasional bacon butty was, to Jill, an acceptable gesture towards Trevor's proletarian roots; but she could not tolerate his apparent need to have a bacon butty every day, in addition to the compulsory cornflakes. She was in the midst of reconstructing her dietary habits around the code words fibre and metabolism. Bacon butties and cornflakes were on the way out, though Trevor was putting up a sturdy defence. 'Take away the cornflakes, where do I get the plastic aeroplanes? It's good for my manipulative skills.'

'Manipulative skills' was another phrase he'd learned from Jill, along with 'role reversal' and 'male oppression'. On the morning after the evening of shelves and cassettes, he was feeling more than a little oppressed, aware of Jill's disapproving glances as he bit into his bacon butty.

'I know what you're going to say,' he said, 'you're going to say bacon butties are really bad for you.'

'Bacon butties are really bad for you.'

'I pay my share of the housekeeping. I have bought the bacon. I have bought the bread. I have prepared the butty. That seems fair to me. What's that stuff you're eating?' He peered into her dish. The contents looked fawn and unfinished.

'Muesli.'

'I bet you're going to tell me it's really good for you.'

'I'm not in the habit of preaching. But yes, it is.'

They lapsed into a tranquil silence. Their early morning verbals were still closer to badinage than battlefield, though Trevor was always the first to seek reassurance. He was the sort of man who needed regular reassurance. Jill often told him there was no other sort of man, but this failed to reassure him. As he rinsed his butty plate and placed it carefully in the dishwasher he asked her: 'Was it like this, being married?'

'Like what?'

'Wittering at each other over breakfast?'

'We weren't wittering. We were simply discussing alternative diets. Being married was different. We shouted at each other. And sometimes we yawned. That's what made me throw him out. The yawning.'

Trevor stifled a yawn as he cleared away the cups and saucers, rinsed them, and placed them in the dishwasher too, in precise accordance with the manufacturer's instructions.

'So, is this better than being married?'

'Yes, Trevor, this is much better.'

He kissed her gently on the top of the head, in precise accordance with chapter four of a book he had found in Jill's library, which ordained that regular bodily contact, however fleeting, was the cement in the masonry of loving relationships, or words to that effect. Trevor Chaplin had become much more lavish in bestowing kisses and cuddles since meeting Jill. Previously, he had felt safer patting dogs than women.

Jill smiled in acknowledgement of the kiss, continued her brooding about 15 down in the *Guardian* crossword, and added a footnote to her earlier statement.

'This is better because it isn't permanent. Any more questions?'

'Yes. What did you do with that tape?'

'Tape?'

'The tape from the weird barman. I can find the jazz tapes, but I can't find the one with those fellers talking about nuclear waste.'

'Why do you want it?'

'I was going to take it back to the pub at lunchtime.'

'No, you're not.'

'OK, I won't bother.'

As they climbed into Trevor's crumpled yellow van, which was now a familiar landmark on the executive estate, Jill explained her theories about the tape. Obviously the weird barman had not intended them to have it. Equally obviously, a recording of men with plummy voices discussing the dumping of nuclear waste in sensitive areas was of considerable political significance.

'I want to know who these people are, where they are planning to dump their filth, and why somebody bugged their conversation.'

'Ask the weird barman. He wears a Greenpeace tee-shirt.'

'He's so efficient he passes on an explosive tape to a couple of complete strangers. People like him aren't to be trusted with confidential information.'

'So he's dumb. So we've still nicked his tape.'

31

'We haven't nicked it. He gave it to us.'

'By mistake.'

The van drove away in the direction of San Quentin High. Its regular presence on the executive street had not gone unnoticed. Opposite Jill's executive house was an executive bungalow, distinguished from its neighbours by having a front lawn with a wishing well, and a five-handed team of garden gnomes. In the bungalow lived the man believed by Jill to be an unfrocked bank manager – an assessment not a million miles away from the truth.

By the time Trevor and Jill arrived at school, the Swinburne policy on incriminating tapes had become clear. She was taking over the operation and the investigation. Environmental politics was her speciality and she would not be moved. Trevor's part in the process was to do as he was told and not ask silly questions.

'Can I ask one silly question?'

'Well – providing it's really silly.'

'Where is the tape now?'

'In a safe place.'

'Thank you,' said Trevor, and they went into school, braced for another day of scholarship and attrition.

Mr Carter walked from the dining hall to the staffroom with the bearing of a man betrayed. He had always been a man who betrayed easily, indeed he quite relished the experience. Compassion and kindness bothered him, so most people, aware of his feelings, concentrated on small betrayals. They wanted him to be content.

He marched across the staffroom, passing a PE specialist contemplating his athlete's foot, two young maths teachers comparing their punk hairstyles, and a neurotic sociology graduate completing a job application. He arrived in the far corner of the room, where he found his target, Trevor Chaplin, crumpled up in a balding armchair, reading the back page of a tabloid and failing to unwrap a package.

'I am betrayed, Mr Chaplin.'

'Tough,' said Trevor, without rancour.

Mr Carter sat down nearby and launched into a speech he had carefully prepared during his long march from the dining hall.

'Do you realize I have just eaten *alone* in the San Quentin Hilton? No Chaplin, no Swinburne to lighten my darkness.'

'What was for dinner?'

'I had grey windsor soup, a sliver of charred animal flesh with potato that had successfully resisted mashing, a small portion of polystyrene with custard and a carafe of the house white. There are two new dinner ladies in the kitchen so it's *nouvelle cuisine*.'

'Sorry,' said Trevor, 'I missed most of that. Having trouble, see.'

'What are you doing, Mr Chaplin?'

'It's my new diet. Fibre and metabolism in wholemeal bread. Triple-wrapped for extra freshness, and really good for you. Except I can't get near the buggers.'

Mr Carter watched with keen interest as Trevor took a chisel from his top pocket and slit the foil open, to reveal two chunky sandwiches, roughly matching his description.

Trevor bit warily into the first sandwich.

'Did Mrs Swinburne make them?' asked Mr Carter, eager as ever for intimate details of anybody's life.

'No. I made them myself. She gave me instructions.'

'And what lies quivering between those slices of wholemeal bread, waiting to do you good?'

'Free-range lettuce, garnished with an occasional peanut.'

His teeth stumbled over the first peanut.

'How is the taste?'

'I haven't found any yet.'

Mr Carter sighed contentedly, happy to have found a little muffled dissatisfaction in a fellow human being. He decided to probe a little further.

'And where is Mrs Swinburne?'

'Out.'

'Really?'

This answer did not satisfy Mr Carter, who liked hard facts, salacious for preference, though he would settle for the odd sliver of slimy innuendo.

'I can see for myself that Mrs Swinburne is not here. I simply want to know where she is.'

Trevor shrugged. He was trying to give it up, with some success, and he made a quiet mental note: that's the first one today.

'I don't know where she is. She's busy. Doing something. Not my business.'

'But Mr Chaplin, you and she are now, let's not mince words, living together. Cohabiting. As the Good Book says, living in sin . . . I assume?'

'We have our share of sin, yes.'

Trevor finished the first sandwich, looked at the second, decided too much goodness might be bad for him, and dropped it in the nearest wastepaper basket.

'All this sin, yet you don't know where she is? Your indifference is too much for me, Mr Chaplin. The only things that make teaching bearable for me are the prospect of early redundancy with a cash payment, and the lunchtimes spent in close proximity to Mrs Swinburne's sensual glow. I need to know where she is.'

'No you don't. You're just a nosey parker.'

'Also I am a nosey parker.'

Trevor embarked on a ten-minute lecture about the nature of human relationships: how they could only prosper and

34

develop if individuals allowed each other areas of privacy; how Jill respected his obsession with jazz, without wishing to intrude upon it; how he respected Jill's obsession with changing the world, without wishing to touch it with a bargepole. It was an impressive performance, based on a long footnote in the same book that recommended bodily contact. He concluded, 'We live together, but we are free and independent people. We leave space for each other.'

'Leave space for each other! What a splendid thought!'

Mr Carter enjoyed the thought, rolling it around his mind, as a wine taster might examine a rare vintage; then, like a wine taster, he spat it out.

'My wife and I leave space for each other,' he said. 'We never speak.'

Despite his elegy on the theme of personal space, Trevor Chaplin knew exactly what Jill was doing. She had taken the van and driven to the Hay Wain to pursue her inquiries into the genesis and exodus of the tape.

She walked into the same saloon bar where she and Trevor had encountered the weird barman and the Beiderbecke strains. Its appearance had not changed. The room was totally deserted, the dartboard locked away in its cabinet and the mould seemingly restored to the pool table. The dust remained on the counter.

Jill rang the bell and waited. She hoped to see the hippy barman appear, though the pervading atmosphere suggested a time-served zombie was equally likely. She could see an open trapdoor and a flight of steps leading down to a gloomy cellar, always the best place to store zombies. To her surprise and relief, there appeared a proper, old-fashioned pub landlady. She was middle-aged, cheerful, with good pump-handle

forearms and a voice that could call 'Time' across continents
and be heard clearly.

'My God!' she said, seeing Jill, 'a customer!'

'Is that unusual?'

'Can't you see, love? It's like carnival night on the Mary
Celeste. Sunday lunchtimes we get the young executives.
Saturday afternoon the kids get legless before they go off to
kick a few heads at the match. Rest of the time, well, it's
your average cathedral precinct, isn't it?'

Though a cheerful atheist, Jill had visited a few cathedral
precincts in her time, absorbing the essential juices of the
environment. Compared with the saloon bar of the Hay Wain
the energy level of, say, Salisbury or Ely, was fairly frenzied.

'What you having, love?' asked the landlady.

'I don't actually want a drink,' said Jill.

'So what is it? Shelter from the storm? Packet of nuts? Or
are you selling something? Don't bother. There's nothing
worth insuring and we've got more religion than we can cope
with.'

Jill realized that here was a woman best dealt with directly
and honestly. It made a refreshing change from school,
where deviousness was the only policy that anybody practised
nowadays.

'I'd like some information, please, about a man who was in
here the night before last. Serving behind the bar. Sort of an
ageing hippy in a tee-shirt and jeans.'

'You mean John?'

'John? Is that his name?'

Despite her candour, this question was clearly a tricky
one.

'I'm not sure that's his name. That's what we call him.
When he started here he said: call me John. I've worked in
pubs all my life, and when fellers say call me John, you can

36

generally be pretty sure they're called something else. Who are you?'

The question emerged sharply, out of left field. It was thrown on target, but without venom.

'My name's Jill Swinburne. Teacher.'

'My name's Bella Atkinson. Landlady of this parish.'

They smiled. Jill decided she fancied a drink.

'And I'll have a vodka-and-tonic, please.'

Bella served the drink with the speed of light and thirty years' experience.

'I'm glad you're a teacher, love. When you started asking questions, I naturally assumed you were from the Revenue, or the DHSS, or worse.'

'Worse?' said Jill. 'There's something worse than the DHSS?'

Bella glanced around the room, verifying its emptiness, an oddly nervous gesture in a woman whose twitchiness quotient was obviously way below the national average.

'We had a feller in, asking questions about John. Big chap, wouldn't give a name, but I could tell he wasn't Clint Eastwood. Didn't tell him anything. Never trust a man without a name.'

'I've given you a name. What will you tell me?'

'I'll tell you what I know. John used to come drinking in here with a group of friends. Beards, duffel coats, CND badges, newspapers you've never heard of. You know the sort of thing.'

'I *am* that sort of thing, Mrs Atkinson.'

'Bella.'

Jill was reassured by this invitation to use the landlady's first name. It was not only men who sometimes required reassurance. Women investigators were the same, and the investigative pulse was beating firmly as Bella continued.

'The rest of his mates stopped coming. I think the lager was politically unacceptable. But John asked me if there was any chance of casual work behind the bar. So I said yes. Nothing on paper. Strictly cash. If anybody asks, he's a friend of the family helping out.'

Jill could not help but ask the obvious question. 'Does the volume of trade justify extra staff?'

'Being as how you've never seen any customers in here?'

'Well . . .'

'In normal circumstances, no. But since the lord and master, the landlord, the man we laughingly refer to as my husband, is generally smashed out of his skull, yes, we need somebody else.'

'But John isn't here now?'

Again Bella glanced around the deserted bar, confirming the obvious for Jill's benefit.

'Haven't seen him since the night before last.'

'That's the night we saw him.'

'You must have done something with him.'

'Never touched him, your worship.'

'So maybe it was the man with no name.'

Jill sipped thoughtfully at her drink, only to discover the glass was empty. 'Oh look,' she said, 'all that nice vodka seems to have gone.'

'Another?'

'No thank you. I have to explain Shakespeare's *Tempest* this afternoon, to a gang of thirteen-year-olds. You need to be sober to do that.'

Bella smiled. 'We are such stuff as dreams are made on, petal.'

Jill crossed from the main door of the Hay Wain to the crumpled yellow van. Bella Atkinson watched her from the window of the bar, a lonely woman marooned with a brewery's marketing policy and a piss-artist husband. Her face was openly curious, tinged with fear of tomorrow and a sweet yearning for days when pubs were loud and smelly and full, brimming with skittles and dominoes and nasal Irish tenors; when everybody knew what to do with a drunken sailor; and when no man was ashamed to give his real name, assuming he was in a state to remember it.

'What's this?' asked Trevor, prodding his meal, as he sat with Jill in the dining area of the executive through-lounge.

'Ratatouille.'

'The rat's OK. Not crazy about the touille.'

'At least you can't make faces with it.'

Trevor had given occasional lectures to Jill about the ethnic purity of traditional Geordie cooking like pease pudding and singing hinnies, but he was certain that they would not stand up to fibre-and-metabolism analysis. He prodded on in silence.

Jill decided it was time for their married game, when they played at husband-and-wife dialogue.

'Did you have a good day at the workbench, darling?' she said, with the carbolic-bright pertness of a kooky heroine in a TV sitcom.

'Kid in Three B chiselled his finger. We fixed it with the first-aid box. It was a good day, really. It's always a good day when we don't have to call an ambulance. What about you, darling?'

The word 'darling' on Trevor's lips always made Jill laugh. It was like the Pope saying 'Gerroff me foot'. Once she had stopped giggling, she answered the question.

'I failed to explain *The Tempest*, I failed to find John the Barman and I failed to bring thirty-three essays home to mark.'

'No essays to mark! You *always* have essays to mark.'

'I'll leave them till Thursday.'

Trevor had spent most of the afternoon persuading himself

39

that he wanted to pass the evening sandpapering shelves; like a Wimbledon champion, he was psyched up for the main event. For Jill to set aside her well-known professional dedication with such a cavalier mention of Thursday was the most unheard-of thing Trevor had ever heard of.

'I'm in a really terrific sandpapering mood,' he protested.

'Sorry. Change of plans.'

Jill stood up, clearing away the plates, cutlery and the unloved residue of the ratatouille.

'What's for pudding?'

'A brisk walk in the park.'

Trevor and Jill walked briskly in the park, but slowed down after the first fifty yards, which were uphill, settling into a relaxed stroll. Jill explained the strategy behind the walk.

'Quite apart from the metabolism, we're going to the pub. I want to see if John's turned up yet.'

'The weird barman?'

'Yes. It seems he's disappeared.'

'Disappeared? Serves him right. He shouldn't have said balls to the witch doctor.'

Lord Chatham once observed that parks are the lungs of the city. He was talking of London parks. In the moonstruck outer limits of Leeds, and in the greater part of the industrial North, parks have a similar function, but the lungs are a touch wheezy. The trees have difficulty in standing up straight, the flowers need dusting and the grass is even browner on the other side of the hill.

The park that lurked between Jill's house and the Hay Wain was originally a gift from a Victorian industrialist of the paternal school: a sylvan oasis where his workers might linger for twenty minutes in the average week, coughing up the dust they had breathed in during the eighty hours spent in

his factories. Later the park was taken over by the munici-
pality, in the name of the people, and the democratically
elected burghers maintained a bowling green, a steady supply
of ducks, and an adventure playground equipped with the
latest swings, roundabouts and climbing frames – claimed by
some sceptics to be a primitive exercise in population control.
Every Sunday, popular selections of taped muzak were played
through a bronchial PA system fastened to the bandstand with
rusty wire.

Trevor Chaplin and Jill Swinburne were walking past the
bandstand, and he was reminiscing about the lost days of his
Geordie childhood when a bandstand meant a real band, with
a fat officious conductor and a crowd of scruffy kids urging
on the bass drummer to greater violence. He was deep in the
trough of nostalgia when Jill noticed the man following them.

'We're being followed,' she said.

'Well, it's a park, isn't it?'

Trevor, though sentimental about the brass bands of his
childhood, was not sentimental about parks. He assumed that
they were thickly populated with lurkers, voyeurs, prowlers,
flashers and permutations of those elements. Being followed
simply confirmed his prejudice where parks were concerned.

Jill insisted that he look back over his shoulder, being
careful not to look as if he were looking back over his
shoulder. He saw what Jill had seen: a man resolutely
following in their footsteps, at a distance of twenty yards.
Outwardly, he did not seem much of a threat. He was
monumentally average, wearing faded jeans, training shoes,
anorak and the haunted air of one who has lived too long
with lost causes.

'Let's go on the swings,' said Jill, grabbing at Trevor's
sleeve.

'I don't want to go on the swings.'

Then he understood the nature of Jill's ploy. A little way

41

beyond the bandstand stood a cluster of kiddies' swings, plus a slide, strictly O-level standard. Those children who survived graduated to the adventure playground at the age of five or thereabouts. By going on the swings, Jill and Trevor would force their shadow to reveal his intentions.

Jill sat on a swing and indicated Trevor should do the same. Trevor hesitated.

'I'd rather go on the slide,' he said.

'Just sit on the swing.'

'I don't like swings. They go too high.'

'Well go on the rotten slide, you big baby!'

Trevor walked round to the slide, climbed the steps at the rear, and slid gracefully down the slide as Jill swung high in the air, without taking her eyes off the man following them. He was obviously foxed by their manoeuvre. He hesitated as he came nearer to the swings, then quickened his pace and walked past them, disappearing beyond the charred remains of the burnt-out tennis pavilion.

Once he was out of sight, Jill jumped off the swing. 'That's enough,' she said, sharply.

Trevor was halfway up the steps of the slide. 'Can't I have another go?'

'No, that's quite enough for one day.'

Jill started walking back in the direction they had come from. Trevor broke into a run to catch up with her.

'Why are we going home? I thought we were going to the pub?'

'I want to be sure whether he's really following us.'

They walked back to the bandstand, then, at Jill's direction, took a left turn in the direction of the oriental garden and goldfish pond. In mid-turn, Jill glanced back, and sure enough the man had emerged from behind the sports pavilion – burnt down some weeks earlier by two students from Three

B who were stated in court to have emotional difficulties –
and was once again pursuing them, albeit reluctantly.

Increasingly, Jill had the feeling that the man was not a
serious threat. She revised her original theory that he was the
big man with no name who had asked questions of Bella in
the pub. Her latest, not entirely serious thought was that this
might be the man's younger and less competent brother. A
discreet touch on Trevor's elbow, and they turned right into
the oriental garden and goldfish pond, a gift to the city from
a twin town in Iceland. How they wrapped it up and sent it
remained a mystery.

It was a small pond, with a thin layer of water lilies and
slime, a low stone wall, a path running round, all sheltered
from the outside world by hedges and semi-exotic flora. There
were leafy nooks with seats in the hedges, where people
might sit, contemplating nature, international friendship and
the prospect of carnal excesses after dark. Trevor and Jill sat
on one of these secluded benches, contemplating none of
these, but waiting for their shadow.

He duly, and nervously, appeared. Trevor and Jill were
well hidden and the man had walked two-thirds of the
circumference of the oriental pond before he saw them, at a
range of two yards, staring at him from their municipal
bench.

'Are you following us?' asked Jill.

'No.'

'Good. In that case, we will go our way and you can go
yours. Good night.'

She and Trevor stood up.

Panic flickered in the man's eyes. He changed rapidly from
a burdened thirty-year-old to a strident ten-year-old seeing
his lollipop move beyond reach.

'Yes,' he said, 'I *am* following you.'

He moved a pace nearer to them. There was still clear

43

space between him and his two quarries. With an uncharacteristic lurch into initiative, Trevor took a further step nearer.

'I should warn you,' he said, 'don't try anything. I've got a black belt.'

The man took two paces backwards. The heels of his training shoes were pressed against the low wall surrounding the pond. Only the wall separated him from water lilies, slime, goldfish and loss of dignity.

'Are you the man with no name?' asked Jill, encouraged by Trevor's show of force.

'Of course I've got a name. I'm called Dave.'

This eased the tension by several degrees; there is a quality to the name Dave that dilutes the terror in most situations, with the exception of Goliath's.

'I don't want to make trouble,' said Dave, 'I'm not into violence. But you've got something that belongs to me. You've got a tape.'

'A tape?' said Jill.

'A tape?' echoed Trevor. 'What sort of tape? Dizzy Gillespie? Charlie Parker? Bix Beiderbecke?'

'You *know* what sort of tape! It should have been passed on to me and it was passed on to you.'

Jill put on her best school ma'am voice: what she sometimes called her Joyce Grenfell touch.

'Why should I pass on a tape, or anything else for that matter, to a total stranger who follows me around a public park? It would be more responsible of me to report you to the police for loitering.'

Dave threw himself on the mercy of the court.

'Look, I don't want any hassles, man . . .'

'I am a woman.'

'There was a cock-up, that's all. We want the tape back. I'm in dead shtuck over this.'

In his agitation, Dave was fiddling with the zip on his

44

anorak. Jill noticed he was wearing a tee-shirt with a CND symbol. Her attitude softened.

'We're all good, decent subversives,' she said.

Trevor protested. 'I'm not.'

His politics were difficult to define. He became a theoretical conservationist when Jill stood at council elections and needed his van, but otherwise was fervently undecided about most social and political issues. He had waited half a lifetime, his vote poised at the ready, for some likely demagogue to offer Art Blakey's band on the rates, or Ellington LPs on the NHS, but was beginning to think himself an idealist. Politically, Jill thought him a clown, and on this occasion, as on so many others, she ignored him. She launched a speech at Dave, aiming right between the eyes.

'I do not admit possession of your tape, or any other tape. But even if I had a tape containing, let us say, confidential information about the future of the planet Earth, do you know what I would do with it?'

'No,' said Dave.

'What would you do with it?' asked Trevor, genuinely interested in the answer, since he had no idea what he would do if the future of the planet landed in his lap. Jill knew exactly what she would do.

'I would make a number of copies of the tape, and place each of them in safe places, as, for example, in six carefully selected banks.'

'Banks?' said Dave, as if it were the first time he had heard of such institutions.

'I thought there were only five banks,' said Trevor, but he was ignored again.

'Since you're not all that hot at following people through public parks,' continued Jill, 'I imagine breaking into a bank vault might stretch your resources a little.'

Dave nodded. 'Banks. Right. Got it. What happens next?'

'I've given you my message. I suggest you take it to your leader.'

Jill's victim shuffled sideways, like a crab practising a foxtrot, eager, it seemed, to be on the road to his leader, bearing the message.

'OK,' he said, 'sorry about, like, the hassle.'

'That's the way it goes, man,' said Trevor.

He and Jill sat down in their chosen nook and watched as Dave left the oriental garden and goldfish pond. He had the air of a man happy to retire from surveillance, assignations and oriental gardens, with or without the gold watch.

'What was all that about?' asked Trevor.

'Tapes.'

'I could tell that but . . .'

'He's not fit to have a tape. He's a complete wimp. Naïve. The sort of man who gives subversion a bad name.'

'What about that other bit? Making copies and putting them in banks?'

'Pack of lies,' said Jill. 'The tape is in a safe place.'

It was clear that Jill would offer no more information concerning the whereabouts of the tape. They sat in silence for a while, contemplating the oriental ambience and the Anglo-Icelandic friendship it celebrated.

'And what was all that stuff of yours about?' asked Jill. 'All that about karate?'

'Karate? I didn't say anything about karate.'

'You told that wimp that you had a black belt.'

'I have.'

Trevor stood up, unfastened his jacket, lifted up his pullover and revealed the black belt that held his trousers up.

'Got it from Marks'.'

She laughed, and took his hand.

'You're wonderful, Trevor.'

46

'We were going to the pub and now you're making duvet eyes at me.'

'Let's go home,' she said.

Peterson watched them. He had watched them enter the park, become aware of Dave and carry out their diversionary action on the swings. He had watched the meeting at the edge of the goldfish pond. Peterson was a keen-eyed watcher, as befits a man who had trained long and hard for the purpose. His leader believed in long, hard training and there were no limitations on time and resources where such training was concerned. Everything he watched, he remembered and duly recorded.

Peterson was over six feet tall, weighed around two hundred pounds, and, by training and temperament, was never over-awed by black belts. He was skilled at concealment, and equally skilled at well-timed intrusions. He lived, happily enough, in the shadows of an uncertain world.

Peterson was the man with no name.

Three

The unfrocked bank manager who lived opposite Jill Swinburne's house watched with his customary drooling interest as his neighbour returned home with her paramour woodwork teacher. He did not know about their adventures in the park. All he did know was that they were finding an assortment of joys in life denied to him. It had always seemed to him that everybody in the world had riches, material, spiritual and yes, dammit, sexual, that appeared only fleetingly in the balance account of his days. It was this same resentment that had caused him to be unfrocked in the first place. He had now moved to phase two in his campaign. If he could not acquire the richness of others by creative accountancy, he would make sure these others ended up as miserable as he. He threw a brace of unconstructive wishes down his well and went into the house to find a pen.

Jill and Trevor settled in their customary places in the living room, Jill curled up on the settee, Trevor slumped in the armchair. Neither could understand the way the other sat down; it looked painful and uncomfortable. Trevor thought Jill sat down like a frog; she thought Trevor sat down like a stick insect. But they had talked it through, and agreed sitting down was an area of private decision and action, and should be left to the individual, like religion, fluoridation and dogs.

'All these years on the planet earth,' said Jill, 'and I have never before been chased by a man in a public park.'

'If they offer you sweets, insist on the coffee cream.'

'I didn't enjoy it!'

Trevor's face brightened as he recalled his moment of triumph.

'But I came to the rescue, didn't I?'

'My hero,' said Jill, flatly.

This was not quite the response Trevor had anticipated. The mood walking home from the park had been one of exhilaration and anticipation. They had met the supreme challenge and they had overcome. An uninhibited celebration in and around the duvet seemed the obvious consequence, but once they had entered the living room, their mood had flattened, the way the bubbles in a bath disappear with the addition of soap.

'Trouble is,' said Jill, 'the guy was such a wimp.'

Trevor could not help but agree. Like Jill, he found macho men as much fun as recycled semolina, but even so, Dave the wimp seemed to set new standards in flimsiness of mind and body. In retrospect, their triumph felt hollow: on a par with buying a return rail ticket and not coming back.

'Any Frascati in the house?' asked Trevor, hoping that booze might rekindle their rapture.

'No.'

'Never mind. You do the coffee. I'll do the music.'

He jumped up, with a reasonable display of energy by Chaplin standards.

'Is it compulsory? I think I'm suddenly into languor.'

'OK, I'll do both. Any requests?'

Trevor crossed to his newly installed shelves, and decided to browse among the bootleg tapes rather than his records, as a means of putting his new filing system to the test.

'Any requests?' he asked again.

'Beethoven? Mozart? Mahler?'

Jill knew the only orchestral music in the Chaplin files was the 1812 Overture, a present from a one-time girlfriend. She had left the price on and it was in old money – twelve shillings and sixpence to be precise. The record was never played because it reminded Trevor of secret humiliations that one day Jill was determined to uncover. In addition, Jill hated the 1812 Overture.

'Try again,' said Trevor.

'What about Scarlatti?'

'I was vaccinated as a child.'

Jill laughed. It was the second time he had made her laugh that evening. Once more would be close to a Swinburne/Chaplin record.

Usually he was pleased when she laughed at his jokes. This time he frowned.

'What's wrong?'

'Have you been looking through these tapes?'

'Of course not. What's wrong?'

She was sufficiently concerned to stand up and cross to where Trevor was crouched, beside his purpose-made tape shelves.

'Somebody's been looking through these tapes. You're sure it wasn't you? You haven't hidden your secret tape here?'

'I keep telling you. My secret tape is secretly hidden in a secret hiding place.'

'In that case, somebody has definitely been here.'

He emphasized the word definitely with an unusual degree of Geordie vehemence. People might break in and steal his money and his property, for what they were worth – probably about ten pounds on the open market – but minor tamperings with his jazz archives constituted first degree original sin. Love me, love my jazz was the Chaplin gospel, and if you don't love it, keep your filthy hands to yourself.

Jill, sensitive to his sensitivity, asked him gently, 'How can you tell?'

'Because these tapes are all filed according to my special system. It's partly alphabetical, partly by subject, partly whims and fancies.'

'Explain.'

'For example, Duke Ellington is filed under E for Ellington, unless it's a live recording, in which case it comes under C for concerts and/or clubs, except when it's a festival when it goes under F for festivals, all of which is overlooked if the record comes under the heading of Trevor's all-time-greats, in which case it's filed under – '

'T for Trevor's all-time-greats,' Jill interrupted, brightly.

'Yes. It's pretty straightforward, once it's explained.'

At various times during their life together, Trevor had explained many matters to her: association football, ship-building on the River Wear, how to distinguish the tenor sax playing of Lester Young from that of Coleman Hawkins, plus various jokes from the repertoire of Bobby Thompson, the great Tyneside comedian. In every case, she ended up under-standing less rather than more, but it was sound sense to pretend otherwise. Therefore she picked her words carefully.

'It's a perfectly simple system, once you understand it, but a stranger would find it incomprehensible? Is that what you're saying?'

'Yes. Somebody's had his filthy hands on this lot. Hey – could it be Dave the wimp?'

'He couldn't break into an envelope.'

The logical conclusion of tampering with the archives arrived in both their heads simultaneously.

'If somebody's been messing with my tapes . . .' began Trevor.

'. . . He, she, it or they must have broken into the house first,' said Jill.

51

They searched the premises, according to the long traditions of detective fiction, looking for telltale hints of forced entry, like broken glass, bloodstains or a forgotten burglar. They found nothing, had coffee, and went to bed.

Under the duvet they lay close together, pretending to read; in Jill's case the latest feminist novel guaranteed to change lives, in Trevor's a massively informative football annual, ostensibly tracing a midfield player from Darlington who had gone to school with his brother. Still the question nagged: who was the mysterious intruder and how had he got in?

'You can open a door with a bit of wire and a credit card,' he murmured.

'Can you?'

'Well I can't, personally, but it can be done.' He thought of somebody who might be able to do it. 'What about Three B?'

All the teachers at San Quentin High regarded Three B as a legendary example of a creative response to the educational scrapheap. Told from birth that they had no hope of academic achievement, even at the level of a CSE pass in shoelace tying, the kids in the class had developed petty vandalism, shoplifting and larceny to levels of sophistication previously unknown among the youth of the parish. Given new sets of parents, any of them could, with the passing years, make a fortune in the City.

'I still don't think it's Three B,' said Jill.

'Why not?'

'First, they're nice kids and they like me. Second, they wouldn't be able to get a credit card, because nobody would give them a reference.'

Though privately he regarded Three B as a tribe of apprentice gangsters, Trevor accepted that the kids, as a group, held Jill in warmth and affection. Trying to debate the issue always ended up with her beating him over the head with a liberal conscience. It also occurred to him that every member of the class probably had six stolen credit cards in each pocket, but he remained silent.

He gave up looking for the lost sportsman from Darlington, and leaned across to put the book down on the bedside table.

'That's nice,' said Jill.

'What?'

'Didn't you notice? A little morsel of bodily contact?'

'My leg was going to sleep.'

'You irresistible romantic fool, you.'

'But I think it's waking up.'

Pretty soon they were both wide awake in all their favourite zones, and thoughts of clandestine tape-recordings, creeping surveillance in public parks and mysterious break-ins were consigned to their proper oblivion. Jill even forgave Trevor's climactic cry of 'Howay the lads!' since her inner voice was echoing the same sentiment, in as near perfect synchronization as makes no difference.

'And afterwards they slept,' said Jill, afterwards.

Next day Mr Carter was laughing again.

He was laughing from the staffroom window and laughing still as they walked into the room, moderately keen to discover what disaster his cheeriness indicated.

'Mr Wheeler wants to see you,' he beamed, through his bi-focals.

'Who? Me? Or him?'

'Both of you.'

'Golly! Up before the beak!' said Jill.

Much of San Quentin High's activity was subjected to an analysis based on public school fantasy. The headmaster's dream, more powerful than Martin Luther King's, of a school after the manner of Eton, Harrow, Rugby or Winchester was matched, and on the whole subverted, by a joint fantasy, shared by Messrs Carter, Swinburne and Chaplin, of a down-at-heel establishment combining elements of boys' comics and BBC cricket commentaries. In this dream-world, Trevor became 'Old Chappers' and life was a sequence of surrealistic incidents: lost tuck boxes, high jinks in the dorm after lights out and going to the sick bay for special treatment from Matron Swinburne, who was famous for her inventive cures. It was a wild dream that kept the drabness at bay.

'And when does old Wheeler want to see us?' asked Jill.

'Immediately.'

'It must be really trivial.'

'I know exactly what it's about,' gloated Mr Carter, 'and that is why I am laughing so immoderately.'

'We'll go immediately in about ten minutes,' said Jill. 'We'll pick up your redundancy money at the same time.'

Fifteen minutes later, Jill and Trevor made their way to the headmaster's study. It was an arduous journey, partly overland, and arrival at the door was by no means an end of the affair. Alongside Mr Wheeler's door was an arrangement of buttons, verbals and coloured lights. The generally accepted translations of the officialese of the notice which, in any case, was mostly masked by diverse graffiti, ran along the following lines. If the red light went on, Mr Wheeler was too deeply occupied with personal dementia or selective betrayal to see anybody; if the amber light went on, he would see people with caution, and members of staff usually entered only if accompanied by a union representative, a lawyer and a priest; if the green light went on, he was prepared to welcome all visitors without fear or favour, which normally indicated that the dementia was at bay and the betrayal had been successful.

Trevor pressed all the buttons on offer, but nothing happened.

'Nothing's happened,' he said.

'When none of the lights go on, it means have you checked you've got a clean driving licence, a valid passport and a positive blood test.'

'Come in,' said the voice of the headmaster.

'That's a clever trick,' said Trevor. 'Is it a tape recording?'

'I'm standing behind you in the corridor.'

Trevor and Jill turned to see Mr Wheeler, standing exactly as he had described. The headmaster had a remarkable facility for moving from A to B without being seen in the act. There were theories in the staffroom about trapdoors and secret passages, about a translocation kit available from the *Observer* and about packages arriving at the school under plain wrapper, postmarked Transylvania. Whatever the explanation, Mr Wheeler had done it again, and without leaving a silvery trail, because Jill checked before she and Trevor followed him into his study.

He sat down behind his desk, pivoted in his large chair, two sizes too big for such a small man, and did not invite Jill and Trevor to sit down.

'Mrs Swinburne, Mr Chaplin . . . I won't mince words or beat about the bush. I want to talk to you about your . . . living arrangements.'

Whenever he threatened to speak directly, it usually took several days to discern what he was talking about. Anxious not to have the discussion overlap into the long summer vacation, Jill and Trevor pushed gently but firmly on his psyche.

'Our living arrangements?'

'I don't think Mrs Swinburne quite understands . . . and nor do I . . . what, with respect, sir . . . you're talking about. Living arrangements?'

55

'Your arrangements for living, as I understand it, together.'

He paused in his pivoting, having used the word 'together', thereby crossing the boundary into normally forbidden territory: sex and related topics left him inarticulate and knotted. He was the sort of man who would blush if the word homeopathic was used in mixed company. Jill, knowing of his limitations, realized she could determine the agenda.

'Together?' she asked, hoping to make him squirm into a more direct accusation.

'Yes. Together. Living . . . together.'

'Mr Chaplin is living at my house until he can find alternative accommodation. His house, as you might know, was demolished recently.'

'They needed the space to make a motorway,' added Trevor, as a helpful footnote.

'And is that wise?'

'You're a car driver, Mr Wheeler, and there's a great deal of congestion on the roads. I know when I'm driving my van to school in the morning, I often think how much better life would be if we had more motorways. In fact, I was only saying to Mrs Swinburne this morning . . .'

'I am not concerned with your van, Mr Chaplin! I am not concerned with motorways!'

It was a regular pattern in confrontations between Trevor and the headmaster: Trevor would start jabbering and Mr Wheeler, driven to stage two distraction, would interrupt, sharply. This sometimes had the merit of revealing the true reason for the summons to interview. Another tip of the iceberg emerged, albeit warily.

'I am not concerned with traffic congestion! I am concerned with members of my staff . . . cohabiting!'

It was the filthiest word the headmaster had used since August 1978 when his then Head Boy had won an Inter-School debating contest, only to be disqualified for using

56

artificial stimulants. Indeed, that was the only time San Quentin High had been anywhere near requiring an Honours Board. Having a former student playing prop forward for Bradford Northern was like having dandruff: it was nothing to be ashamed of but you didn't inscribe it in Roman lettering in a prominent place.

'Cohabiting?' said Jill.

Trevor looked at her, curiously. 'We don't cohabit all that often, do we?'

'Far be it from me to preach at anybody about personal morality,' said Mr Wheeler, a sure sign he was going to preach at them about personal morality. 'But it upsets people.'

'I'm sorry, Mr Wheeler,' said Jill, sure of her ground, 'but I always thought how people behave in their private lives is their own business. Private, you might say. And may I ask: what is *it*, and who are these people that it upsets?'

The headmaster took a deep breath, aware of yet more filthy words lurking in the wings, daring him to speak them.

'It, in this context, is two of my staff cohabiting, with all that it implies. These people, as you call them, are members of the community who are unhappy about such behaviour.'

Jill chanced her arm.

'Phone calls and anonymous letters?'

She said it quietly, almost as an aside. It struck home.

'Both.'

There was an uneasy pause as Mr Wheeler realized he had shown his hand, and a pretty shabby hand it was too, even by his subterranean standards. Trevor was indignant.

'Who's been sending anonymous letters?'

'Think about it,' said Jill.

He thought about it and grunted acknowledgement.

'Mind you,' Jill added, 'I bet I know who's been sending them.'

'Who?' asked the headmaster, every inch a tabloid page

57

three man beneath his puny and ambitious frame. Mr Carter was fond of observing that Mr Wheeler, though small, was quite nastily made.

'Who?' echoed Trevor, for more honourable reasons, like self-preservation.

'That unfrocked bank manager who lives across the road. He's had it in for me ever since I put a CND sticker on one of his garden gnomes.'

It was clear from the headmaster's twitchy reaction that he had full knowledge of the identity of his anonymous informer. The strongest proof of his guilt was the instant evasion: 'The source of the complaints is irrelevant. The relevant question is: what are you going to do about it?'

'Nothing?' Trevor and Jill suggested, simultaneously. Jill elaborated on the theme.

'Our teaching is well up to standard. We get on with our work and we get on with our private lives, and we let other people do the same.'

'I agree with you in principle,' said Mr Wheeler, pivoting his chair forty-five degrees anti-clockwise. They knew that his agreement in principle meant a disagreement in practice amounting to total war. 'But in practice,' he continued, 'I would like to see a positive gesture from the two of you.'

'We could blow up his wishing well,' Trevor suggested, always quick with a positive gesture.

Mr Wheeler ignored him. Trevor shrugged. Their relationship had prospered on this basis for years.

'I am looking for a positive gesture towards the school and the local community. There is a notice in the staffroom, inviting volunteers from members of staff to accompany myself and the school trip to Holland in the summer holidays. Perhaps you'd be good enough to sign your names and we'll forget this other little matter of personal morality.'

The after-match summary of Mr Wheeler's tactics took place in the canteen over lunch. Trevor and Jill needed the comfort of Mr Carter's cynicism, thoroughly boiled cabbage and the ambience of a steelworks on double-time.

Reactions to the headmaster's cunning were varied, even contradictory.

Mr Carter laughed.

Trevor said, 'The shifty, spineless, double-crossing little turd.'

Mr Carter laughed again.

Jill said, 'There is no problem.'

'Of course there's a problem,' said Trevor. 'We're in great danger of having to go on a cheap school trip to Holland with Mr Wheeler and a bunch of monsters. I'll ring my mother. Arrange for her to be ill.'

Mr Carter laughed again.

Jill repeated, 'There is no problem.'

Mr Carter stopped laughing. When Jill Swinburne spoke with such cool conviction, there was a strong possibility of truth and logic in her mind. Perhaps there was no problem, in which case there was no point in his laughing. He was a paid-up member of the philosophical club that believed laughter was a defence mechanism against the world's pain; take away the agony, the despair, the anguish, and on the whole there was nothing to laugh at at all.

'Tell me, my dear,' he asked, in an anxious tone, 'why is there no problem?'

'Because there won't be a school trip if none of the kids want to go. The last time we looked at their notice board the only volunteers were Francis of Assissi and sergeant Bilko.'

'I believe Stanley Baldwin and Champion the Wonder Horse have added their names since then,' said Mr Carter, but the sparkle had left his eyes. Jill had sprung the trap and a summer of relative freedom beckoned her and Trevor, with mists and mellow fruitfulness to follow.

Trevor smiled broadly, for the first time since 'afterwards' the previous night. He stood up.

'I've changed my mind. I'm going to have jam sponge with extra custard.'

'If you're prepared to believe that it really is jam . . .' warned Jill.

'You'll have it on your conscience for the rest of your life,' added Mr Carter.

Trevor took two paces in the direction of the self-service hatch, then collided with Yvonne Fairweather, one of the sharpest fixers in Three B. She had the looks of the young Anna Neagle, the business acumen of Al Capone and the reticent charm of Spike Jones and his City Slickers.

'Hey sir, innit great?'

'The jam sponge?'

Yvonne marched past him to speak to Jill.

'Hey miss, innit great?'

Trevor abandoned thoughts of pudding and took two paces back to the table, as Jill and Mr Carter waited for an explanation. Animation and enthusiasm were unfamiliar items in the heart of Three B. There had to be a reason.

'Ideas of greatness do not dwell happily within the walls of this school,' said Mr Carter, 'and we would welcome your shining a modest torch in the darkness of our bewilderment.'

'You what?'

'What do you mean by innit great?' asked Jill.

'You and sir going on the school trip. I just put my name on the list.'

'Why?' said sir and miss in unison.

''Cos I wanna go on it.'

'That's not much of an ambition for a bright kid like you,' said Trevor.

'But you and Mrs Swinburne are going, so it's bound to be a good laugh, innit?'

'Yes,' agreed Mr Carter, easing his way into a good laugh.

Jill frowned. 'A good laugh?'

'Everybody thinks so, miss. There's dozens of names on the list now we know you and sir are going. Most of Three B wants to go.'

Trevor sat down, thoughts of jam sponge evaporating in the heat of this new crisis.

'Can we just get this clear,' he said. 'Are you trying to tell us that we, that is, me and Mrs Swinburne, are popular?'

'Yes sir. Especially Mrs Swinburne. She's magic.'

The magical Mrs Swinburne began to regret the long years spent building mutual trust with her students.

'So we've got until the end of term to make you hate us?' she suggested.

'No chance,' said Yvonne, laughing, 'we all think you're dead great, you two.'

As sure as hell, Trevor Chaplin was not born dead great, had not achieved dead greatness, and was very nervous of having dead greatness thrust upon him, especially by Three B.

'Just as a matter of interest . . . why do you think we're . . . dead great?'

'It's a bit personal, you know, like.'

'Nothing can hurt them now,' said Mr Carter, so happy he was seriously considering having some jam sponge and custard.

'Well sir, miss,' stumbled Yvonne, briefly inhibited, 'you see, it's like you two living together when you're not married. And Mr Wheeler thinks it's terrible and hates you. And you two don't give a toss. And that's dead great. We think you're a very good example to us all.'

The notion of Chaplin and Swinburne as a good example

stopped all three of the teachers in their tracks. Mr Carter wiped his bi-focals with his handkerchief. They had steamed up in the heat of revelation.

'My dear,' he said, as if auditioning for a cheap remake of Goodbye Mr Chips, 'we never imagined that any member of Three B was capable of following an example. Nor did we imagine that any member of the staff had the moral stature to set one. Both ideas are totally ludicrous.'

Yvonne fastened on the one word in the speech that made any sense to her.

'Well it isn't moral, is it, sir? That's what makes it magic. That's what makes them dead great.'

'Go back to your table, Yvonne,' said Jill, 'have a glass of water and bring me an apple first thing in the morning.'

'Yes miss,' Yvonne replied. 'See you round the back of the windmill in old Amsterdam.'

Yvonne returned to her table. She clearly reported the gist of the conversation. It was followed by loud laughter and a raucous closing-time-style medley of songs from the film 'Hans Christian Andersen'. Jill made a mental note: remind Three B that there is a difference between Holland and Denmark, and try to think of some famous Dutchman they might have heard of. It would not be easy.

On that summer evening in the moonstruck outer limits of Leeds, three men, men who normally veered between surly silence and black misery, were happy.

Mr Wheeler sat alone in his living room, smiling at his triumph over Trevor and Jill. To him they were not dead great; they were dead awkward. His wife was at her night-class in Industrial Archeology. He encouraged her to go to evening classes, to expand her mind to the dimensions required of the wife of a public school headmaster, in the dream that still flickered periodically in the wee small hours of his mind. It was also better than having to talk to each other. Solitary – that was the best way to gloat over a victory. He would have a small glass of sherry, top up the bottle with water and suck a peppermint before she returned.

Mr Carter dozed contentedly in front of his television set. The sound was turned down. It was summer and BBC1 was giving him a second chance to see a rerun of some long-forgotten ice-skaters. The alternatives were a game show on ITV, in which self-confessed salt-of-the-earth people were encouraged by a near-elderly juvenile lead with thirty-two teeth to leap around like dervishes in the quest for a micro-wave oven, and on BBC2 and Channel 4, interchangeable documentaries about people's rights being analysed in work-shop situations. Mr Carter was happy because he relished the ups and downs, the ebbs and flows, in the life of his colleagues Trevor Chaplin and Jill Swinburne. They were like characters in a daily strip cartoon, prepared especially for him, and like all such characters, to him they were immortal. That was the source of his secret smile.

The unfrocked bank manager was smiling, as he walked the boundaries of his estate. He was probably the first anonymous telephone caller in the history of sneakery to have had a reply. It went without saying that he did not think his neighbours were dead great. He thought them a creeping menace, whose subversive tendencies and disreputable moral-ity were undermining all that was most precious in our island heritage. They were responsible, alone and unaided, for inner city riots, picket-line violence and inflationary tendencies in the economy. On reflection, a holiday trip to Holland was a smaller punishment than he would have wished, but it was a step in some sort of direction, and he hoped it was the right one.

He patted his lawn, stroked his wishing well, then paused

as he was about to offer a friendly greeting to his garden gnomes. On the largest of these there was a sticker reading: MAKE LOVE, NOT WAR. Not only that, it was fastened, appropriately enough, on the gnome's fly. What made it worse, there was a look in the gnome's face that indicated he was ready to start immediately, and, though it could only have been a trick of the summer light, the trousers were bulging quite eagerly too.

The unfrocked bank manager did what he had never done before. He kicked his gnome. Then he went indoors to bathe his foot.

Trevor and Jill were unaware of the physical and emotional unheavals they were causing across the shire. They were concentrating on their meal. It was Trevor's turn to prepare dinner and they were having cheese-on-toast, as they always did when it was his turn to prepare dinner. Since moving in on a permanent basis he no longer used white sliced bread and pre-sliced cheese, but the essential strategy was unaltered.

'Goody goody, cheese-on-toast,' said Jill.

'I've had to learn a lot of new things since I became your cohab. I've had to learn new names for every meal. You can't expect me to learn new cooking as well.'

There had been long debates about the semantics of eating. In Trevor's world there were three fixed meals and one optional: breakfast, dinner, tea and fish-and-chips or chicken vindaloo if you'd been to the pub. In Jill's world these became breakfast, lunch and a floater that was sometimes dinner, sometimes supper. An element called afternoon tea occasionally sneaked in under the fence. For the moment, Jill's definitions held the balance of power, since it was her house.

'Tell you what,' said Trevor, 'why don't we think positive?'

It was a phrase he had picked up from watching too many television interviews with soccer managers.

'You want me to throw this away?'

'Not about the meal. About Holland.'

Until that moment, they had both avoided the subject of the school trip. They hoped it would leave them alone and go away.

'You can't be positive about it,' Jill said. 'It's like looking on the bright side of dry rot or boils.'

Trevor insisted and soon, like much of their activity, it turned into a non-competitive game.

'Holland is very flat,' said Trevor, 'therefore there are no hills to fall off. Therefore it is a very safe place to visit. Your turn.'

'There's a famous red-light district in Amsterdam, or Rotterdam, one of the dams, and we could sell Mr Wheeler's body into white slavery, in the cause of unspeakable perversions. Your turn.'

'There are some good footballers in Holland.'

'Footballers don't count as good things. What about art?'

'Oh yes. Art's a good thing. Dead great.'

Trevor stood up and crossed to the sink to fill the kettle, as Jill listed the forthcoming attractions of Dutch art.

'Dutch art. Interiors. People standing in rooms. Or sometimes sitting.'

'Sounds pretty exciting, that. Wow.'

'Knock it off, smartarse. You think of something. What about jazz musicians?'

This gave Trevor something to think about while he made the coffee. It became a gentle soliloquy, as Jill picked up the *Guardian*. When Trevor was improvising on a jazz theme, even at her invitation, she liked to have some alternative activity close at hand.

'Dutch jazz musicians,' he mused. 'That's quite tricky.

There's Bengt Hallberg but he's a Swede . . . there was Django Reinhardt, but he was a Belgian gypsy . . . and Neils-Henning Ørsted Pederson, but he's from Denmark . . .'

By the time Jill had moved into the living area of the executive through-lounge Trevor had progressed to: 'Albert Mangelsdorff, he makes farting noises on the trombone but he's a German.' And by the time Trevor followed, carrying the coffee tray, he accompanied his elegant servility with: 'Not forgetting Alexander von Schlippenbach, but I'm not sure what he does or where he comes from.'

Jill stared at him.

'I've forgotten what the question was.'

Before he could explain that it was all a quest for legendary Dutch jazz musicians, and he was beginning to think it was a non-existent species, the doorbell rang. For once, Jill almost hoped it was an insurance salesman or a religious zealot.

Trevor answered the door. On the doorstep was Peterson, the man with no name.

'Mr Chaplin?'

'Yes.'

'Mrs Swinburne at home?'

'Yes.'

'Please don't make any fuss. I am strong, highly trained and merciless and I am coming into this house.'

'In that case you'd better come in.'

Trevor led Peterson into the living area.

'This gentleman would like a word with you. Or me?'

'Both, probably.'

Jill could tell at a glance that Peterson was not selling religion or insurance, though he could well be into zealotry. He filled most of the room not already occupied by furniture, Jill, Trevor, shelves, records, tapes and the *Guardian*. He loomed over his context.

'Sit down, Mr Chaplin. Sit down, Mrs Swinburne.'

They did as they were told. Peterson remained standing. He loomed even more; he probably had a Ph.D in looming.

'I do not waste time. I do not waste words. I do not waste energy. I want that tape.'

'We've got hundreds of tapes,' said Trevor.

'Music!'

Peterson looked across at the tapes on the shelves, spitting out the word music as if it were toxic. Jill asked the obvious questions.

'Have you already looked? Was it you that broke in?'

His silence implied yes.

'I know who you are,' said Jill. 'You're the man with no name.' She was convinced this was the man who had visited the Hay Wain, asking questions about John the barman. The accusation startled their visitor, albeit for a split second only.

'Of course I've got a name. My name's Peterson.'

'Peterson?'

'It will serve our purposes.'

'Do we have some purposes?' asked Jill, who was beginning to resent not holding the initiative in the conversation. But Peterson was stronger opposition than Trevor, Mr Carter, Mr Wheeler or even Yvonne Fairweather.

'You are in possession of a tape. We want it back. End of story.'

'It isn't here,' said Jill.

'Where is it?'

'There was a chap followed us in the park. Was he one of your lot?'

'I doubt it.'

'And the bloke in the pub,' said Trevor, afraid that his silence might be interpreted as fear. He was frightened but did not want it to show.

'Mr Chaplin, Mrs Swinburne, there are two sorts of people. People like you and the wimp in the park – '

'Interesting,' said Trevor. 'We thought he was a wimp as well.'

Peterson was not happy about being interrupted and carried on as if nothing had happened. Obviously, in the twilight zones of his world, off-duty woodwork teachers were zero-rated.

' – the wimp in the park, the do-gooder who serves behind the bar in that pub. You are all alike. People who have no right to be dealing in tapes, and information that is no concern of theirs.'

'And the other sort of people?' asked Jill, pretty sure of the answer.

'People like me. People who have a right to the tape. People who have a right to the information. We want that tape back. I will break bones if necessary.'

He said nothing else. Jill could think of no adequate reply. Trevor did a rapid calculation on the number of bones in the human body.

'Well?' Peterson was coldly eager for a response.

Jill stood up. 'Do you have a car?'

He nodded.

'We'll lead and you can follow. I'll show you where the tape is.'

As Trevor drove along the main road leading from the executive estate to the city centre, he inquired of Jill, with a deal of anxiety, 'This isn't a car chase, is it?'

'No.'

'That's a relief.'

He glanced in the mirror. Peterson was following the van in a powerful black saloon car, the kind that is always left with its engine running.

They both hated car chases, Jill because they were boring, Trevor because he did not like driving fast and his yellow van was not designed for speed anyway.

'Where are we going?'

'Take the next on the right.'

'That leads to the canal.'

'Guess where we're going.'

There are over two thousand miles of inland navigable waterways in the United Kingdom. Once upon a time they formed the backbone of an Industrial Revolution, the British Empire and related institutions such as poverty, degradation and rickets. The Blackwater Canal, buried deep in the heart of downtown Leeds, had never been the backbone of anything. It was a tributary of a tributary, abandoned when the builder was taken bankrupt one Tuesday early in the nineteenth century. There was in existence a Blackwater Canal Trust, dedicated to revitalizing it, lining its banks with folk singers and stalls selling pottery and hand-woven health food, but this was still in the committee stage.

The Blackwater Canal was not navigable and had never been navigated, since it went nowhere that could not be reached ten times as quickly on foot. A small, hump-backed bridge spanned its dark and sludgy waters. Trevor stopped his van on the bridge, and waited for Peterson's car to do the same.

The three people left their vehicles and leaned over the parapet, gazing down at the canal. The ooze glared back at them. Though it had never been navigated, the people, resourceful and resilient as ever, had found a use for the canal. They dumped their surplus requirements in it: unwanted furniture, dead cats, old perambulators, surplus drunks. It was not a pretty spot. Doctors recommended that even a casual glance at its surface should be followed by a course of anti-tetanus injections.

Peterson, Jill and Trevor stared at the black, glacial surface with awe: there was majesty in this muck.

'The tape's in there?' said Peterson.

Jill nodded, then explained her rationale.

'You must have done your homework. You know the sort of league I'm in. Conservation. Women's rights. The environment. Blue whales. Flabby, liberal-minded and wet, by your standards.'

'Right.'

'So totally by accident I come to be in possession of a tape. *Your* tape. I haven't a clue what it's about, except it's top security. High-level stuff. Right out of my class. I did what any flabby, wet, liberal-minded woman would do. I panicked and threw the tape into the canal. Was that sensible?'

'That was very sensible,' said Peterson.

She had said exactly what he wanted to hear. He turned, climbed into his car, and drove away.

'Did you really chuck it in the canal?' asked Trevor.

'No. That was all bollocks. The tape's in a safe place.'

'I'd rather you didn't tell lies to a fellow like that. He strikes me as a very nasty man.'

'And I, Mr Chaplin, can be a very nasty woman.'

'Well, yes, I know that but . . .'

'Pardon?'

They drove to the Hay Wain, partly to celebrate Jill's triumph over the man with no name, partly because Trevor needed a drink to settle his stomach. He had a lurking fear that bones might yet be broken, and was allergic to fractures. Jill's cheerful reassurances did not help.

'I know about these mysterious men who appear on doorsteps. They're all macho men, terrified inside. Most of them have serious personality defects.'

'Like Charlie Crippen.'

'You've got to admit, it was a good wheeze, pretending I'd

thrown it in the canal. It was all that talk of Holland. That's what gave me the idea.'

'The Dutch Swing College Band!'

'I'm sorry?'

'Before that bloke came, I was trying to think of jazz musicians from Holland, and I just remembered. The Dutch Swing College Band. They're from Holland. They're a band.'

'Is that why they're called Dutch?'

They arrived at the Hay Wain to find it as crowded and hectic as Oliver Goldsmith's village. Mrs Atkinson was behind the bar, with an old copy of *Spare Rib* propped up against the pump handles. She was pleased to see them. She would have been pleased to see anybody, barring the VAT man.

'Hello dear,' she said to Jill. 'The usual? Vodka-and-tonic? And for your gentleman friend?'

'Pint of bitter please,' said Trevor, a little worried at being described that way. It made him sound like a commercial traveller.

'And something for yourself,' added Jill.

'I'll just have a glass of water, on the rocks.'

Glasses charged, account paid, the three of them remained in a friendly group, either side of the bar.

'Cheers,' said Trevor, raising his glass.

'Rest in peace,' said Bella.

Jill and Trevor were surprised by this response. Even drinking water, Bella was the sort of woman you would expect to say 'Bottoms up', or 'All the best' or 'Up yours'. Jill, in her turn, was the sort of woman to question this brand of inconsistency.

'Rest in peace?' she queried.

'Didn't you know?'

They shook their heads. They certainly did not know. They did not even know what it was they did not know about.

71

'Your musical friend, John the barman. I had a phone call this evening, saying he wouldn't be in for work. Not tonight. Not ever again.'

'Not ever again? As in . . . death?' asked Jill.

'Seems like he's pulled his last pint, dear.'

Trevor was aghast.

'But he was a jazz fan!'

In the Chaplin philosophy of life and death, jazz people were, by definition, immortal.

'Can't help that, dear. That's what the man said. Finito. Kaput. R.I.P. No extra time. Last orders.'

Bella's soliloquy was beginning to sound like the Python dead parrot sketch, so they took their drinks to a corner table to reflect on the frailty and mortality of the human race, with special reference to John the Barman, illicit tapes, the dumping of nuclear waste and Peterson, the man with no name. Trevor turned to Jill, with a face as serious as she could ever remember.

'I have a suggestion to make, pet. Get that tape from its safe place, wherever it is, and chuck it into the canal. Tonight.'

Four

'The story so far,' said Trevor.

It was breakfast time, the morning after the night of Peterson, the Blackwater canal and the reported death of John the barman. They had not returned to the canal to throw the tape into its dank maw. Instead they had discussed the situation in depth and agreed a common policy: they would talk about it tomorrow.

Now it was tomorrow and they were talking about it.

'The story so far,' said Jill. 'It all began when Trevor and Jill went into a pub and the barman played some jazz instead of muzak and he said he would let Trevor have some tapes of that trumpet player chap.'

'Bix Beiderbecke, and he played cornet, not trumpet.'

'Whereupon six tapes were delivered, five containing jazz and one containing a clandestine recording of top security loonies discussing the dumping of nuclear waste in this area.'

'Whereupon we were chased by a wimp in the park and pursued to our home by Peterson, the man with no name. Whereupon you convinced him you'd chucked the tape in the canal. Whereupon we went to the pub and the landlady said John the barman had joined the great big band in the sky.'

'That's enough whereupons.'

Jill started regrouping the components that made up breakfast.

'What are you doing?' asked Trevor.

'I'm sorting out the goodies from the baddies.'

She placed the muesli and an empty yoghurt carton at one side of the table.

'That's you and me. We're goodies.'

She placed the jug of skimmed milk alongside them.

'That's Dave the wimp. He means well so he's a goody as well.'

She placed the carton of grapefruit juice by the milk jug.

'That's John the barman. He's a goody.'

'Except he's dead. He *was* a goody.'

Trevor placed the grapefruit carton respectfully on its side, whistling a short fragment from the Funeral March.

Grapefruit juice, pure, unadulterated and containing no chemical additives, poured all over the table.

'Idiot child!' yelled Jill, as Trevor ran for a cloth, adding as he mopped up the mess, 'But it's something we should check.'

'How can you check grapefruit juice?'

Jill placed the sugar basin on the opposite side of the table. It contained white sugar. It was the last bastion of Trevor's campaign to carry on eating food that was bad for him, roughly equivalent to people who pretend they smoke an occasional cigarette or who only do unspeakable things until they need glasses.

'The sugar basin represents Peterson, who is the only fully certified baddy that we know about so far.'

'Three on to one. He's got no chance. Except he says he can break bones and I believe him. Also we think he bumped off John the barman.'

'Hmmm.'

Whenever Jill said 'Hmmm' the best plan was to find important business to attend to elsewhere and immediately.

74

The sound was heavy with short-term and long-term planning, lucidly assessed and ready for instant application.

'We have to do three things today,' she announced to Trevor as they drove to school.

'We have to go to school and educate the younger generation, preparing for a full and creative adult life.'

'All right. Four things.'

It was an unusual day in the pattern of San Quentin High. Trevor Chaplin had a double free period in the morning and Jill Swinburne had a double free period in the afternoon. In theory, with the massive cuts in education spending, designed to make the nation leaner and fitter and more competitive in world markets, there should no longer have been any minutes in the day when teachers were not teaching. But San Quentin High had an almost unique self-correcting mechanism whereby student absenteeism exactly balanced the decrease in the numbers of staff, so that every teacher retained the same number of free periods. Theoretically, these enabled teachers to refresh their minds, read significant books, brood on mind-expanding projects or just sit quietly and think a few fine thoughts. In practice it was a good skive.

All these calculations formed the background to Jill's 'Hmmm'. She did not 'Hmmm' lightly.

Thus it became the Day of the Three Things, not counting the education of the young.

Trevor thought on these things during morning assembly, an institution preserved by Mr Wheeler in the face of mountainous evidence that it caused everyone else in the school extreme rectal pain. The day's assembly had the standard ingredients: a raucous version of 'Eternal Father', an inaudible reading from the First Book of Kings, mumbled by a reluctant prefect called Spike, and a tirade from the headmaster about the nature of original sin and how it made people smash up the girls' lavatories. As usual, he asked the guilty ones to own up and as usual nothing happened.

Also as usual, Trevor daydreamed through the entire charade, but today the dreaming was to a purpose. Jill had given him the task of checking out the background details to the alleged death of John the barman during his double free period. She had not told him how to do it. He was left to his own devices and in the area of investigating mortality, his store of devices ran low. Nonetheless, death-checking was his Thing.

Jill's Thing was a visit to the Old Folks' Home. She had not told him why she was going to the Old Folks' Home.

Assembly dragged to its close and as the final 'Amen' drained away into history, Trevor realized she had not told him about the third Thing they had to do.

'What's the third thing?' he said, as they left the hall.

'We have to go to the supermarket.'

By mid-morning, Trevor still had no idea how a woodwork teacher was supposed to investigate violent death, but aware of Jill watching him from the staffroom window, he walked to the yellow van with as much purpose as he could summon. He was concentrating so hard on looking purposeful that he did not see Mr Wheeler watching from the shadows. The man travelled in a permanent shroud of shadow. He could probably have stepped from a shadowy nook in the middle of the Nevada desert.

'Leaving early, Mr Chaplin?' he asked.

Trevor was skilled at Wheeler-evasion.

'Just popping out on a quick errand of mercy.'

'Mercy, Mr Chaplin?'

'Yes. Mercy.'

One of Trevor's favourite jazz pieces was a soul song called

76

'Mercy, Mercy, Mercy' by Eddie Jefferson and Joe Zawinul and as he and Mr Wheeler traded the word, the tune started echoing around his head. But there was no music in the headmaster; only sound and fury, seeking an outlet.

'Is there some reason for this sudden lurch into the spiritual, Mr Chaplin?' he asked, spikily, his small body arching like a question mark.

Trevor decided the best tactics were to play on the man's best or worst instincts, according to your point of view.

'Yes, Mr Wheeler. My reason is the sudden and untimely death of a close and valued friend.'

Saying it, Trevor reflected that John the barman was so close a friend, he didn't even know his second name, but he was, or had been – according to the exact state of his health – a jazz fan and that was more important a factor than surnames. Talk of death certainly impressed the headmaster.

'I see. Well, you'd better be on your way.'

'Right then.'

'Blessed are the merciful, for they shall obtain mercy, Mr Chaplin.'

'So I've been told.'

Trevor waited to see whether Mr Wheeler was going to supplement his benediction with a swift laying on of hands, the hearing of confession or an oil check; but nothing else was forthcoming, spiritual or temporal. Trevor climbed into his van and drove off, he knew not where, in pursuit of his Thing.

He rehearsed the speech that had begun to form in his mind during the school assembly.

'Good morning. You don't know me. My name is Trevor Chaplin, and I'm sorry to bother you but there's this man called John and I think he's dead, but I'm not sure how it happened and I'm not even sure whether John is his real name or whether he's really dead. He used to work in a pub called the Hay Wain, maybe you know the place, beer's like platypus-piss, and he liked jazz, especially Bix Beiderbecke. Oh yes, and he had a beard. Bit scruffy but a good lad. You must know him.'

He hesitated. It sounded nonsense, and after a pause, he continued, 'Why are you calling the police?'

Maybe it was Jill's idea, but it was madness. He had never investigated death in his life and his only practical suggestion – to go to the police – had been forbidden by Jill because of the political implications of the case and because, according to Alfred Hitchcock, the police were boring. In any case, they were both on the police computer and, a year earlier, had been responsible for a senior officer being discharged with a badly tarnished reputation and decimated pension.

This being so, Trevor was a man with a long and complicated question and nowhere to take it. He found an Eddie Jefferson cassette and hid inside his music as he drove around, looking for possible information sources.

He found a cemetery. In the cemetery was a man, digging a hole. His name was Charlie. Trevor parked the van, and walked along the gravel path, seeking the courage to put his carefully rehearsed question.

'Good morning,' he said. 'You don't know me. My name is Trevor Chaplin and I'm sorry to bother you but . . .'

'You're not bothering me, sunbeam. People don't talk to me as a rule.'

Charlie was a jovial man in his forties. There was mischief in his eye and a Woodbine on his lower lip. It was difficult to tell how tall he was because he was standing in the hole, but his width was impressive.

Greeted with such warmth, Trevor tried to show a keen and intelligent interest in the man's work.

'That's a really good hole you're digging.'

'Ta. It's coming along nicely. The ground helps. This

78

corner of the cemetery, your soil's more welcoming. Over yonder's like Aberdeen granite, but this is grand stuff. Warm and welcoming. You can pull it round you like a blanket.'

'Is it for anybody in particular? The hole?'

Despite Charlie's friendly disposition, Trevor was nervous about putting the question so directly: the cemetery was owned and run by the local authority and curiosity about the identity of the deceased could well have contravened several byelaws. He need not have worried.

'You mean who's going in it?'

'Yes, that's what I mean.'

'No. They never tell me nothing. Just how many holes and how big. I've complained about it. It'd be nice to do it more personal, made-to-measure . . . sort of bespoke . . . instead of just whacking out the holes . . .'

'Wholesale?' suggested Trevor.

'Aye, that's right.'

Charlie laughed. He enjoyed Trevor's joke. He seemed the sort of man who would enjoy jokes at any level, without fear or favour. Then, as if concerned that his attitude might be upsetting his visitor, the face edged into near-solemnity.

'Mind you, it's worse in winter. Frost in the ground. Makes the digging harder. And of course, that's your busy time. Bad weather. People die in larger numbers. We generally have the rush after Christmas. But it's steady. Not many steady jobs these days. Are you in work?'

'Yes, I'm a teacher.'

'Oh, we've got a lot of teachers here.'

He looked across the ranks of headstones, great and small, ancient and modern, spruce and decaying, staking their claims in the hereafter.

'You've got a lot of everything,' said Trevor.

'Yes, we got the bloody lot here. Funny really. This is where it all ends up. After all the drinking and the voting and the insurance men and the odds-on favourites that finish fourth. It all ends here. You have to laugh.'

Trevor was fascinated by this glimpse of Charlie's life style and wondered whether he was interested in jazz. He never found out, because Charlie added, without pause for breath, 'You could try the Registrar's.'

'Eh?'

'Births, Deaths and Marriages. If you're inquiring about, pardon the expression, some body in particular, you could try the Registrar's. They keep lists of all the runners and riders.'

There was a branch of the Registrar's within a quarter of a mile of the cemetery. By the time Trevor arrived, Eddie Jefferson was singing a version of 'Body and Soul' based on the famous Coleman Hawkins solo. It felt appropriate.

Mr Dawson the registrar was smiling as he and Trevor sat down either side of his desk. The smile appeared to be sellotaped in position.

'Now then sir, is it a birth, a death or a marriage we are confronted with?'

'A death.'

Dawson slid open a drawer, took out a death certificate, unscrewed his fountain pen, and prepared himself for action. The smile was overlaid with two coats of compassion.

'First, may I offer my deepest sympathy, Mr . . .'

'Chaplin.'

'Mr Chaplin. If you could just tell me the name of the deceased.'

'I think his name's John.'

'I shall need the full name.'

Trevor launched into a variation on his rehearsed speech. He had planned it during the silence in the waiting room.

'I'm not here to register a death. I'm here to see whether anybody else has. I've heard a rumour that somebody has died. He used to work behind the bar in my local pub. He's got a beard. *Had* a beard. I think his name's John, and I wondered if you could have a quick check in your files to see if it matches anything that . . .'

Dawson had the look of a man running to catch a bus and just failing.

'I'm sorry?'

'This chap called John has died. We think. Somebody told us he died. Except we're not sure. And we don't know his second name. He had a beard.'

'When people register deaths, Mr Chaplin, they very rarely tell us whether or not the deceased had a beard. It isn't a necessity in law.'

The glaze on the smile showed signs of cracking; the gentle compassion crept into hiding, reserved for a more deserving customer.

'He was an old and valued friend,' said Trevor, hoping the line that had worked with Mr Wheeler might do the same with this obviously softer touch.

'How long had you known him?'

'Almost a week.'

All pretence disappeared. The smile became unfixed and was replaced by alarm laced with panic. There was nothing in Dawson's statute book to cover this eventuality. Trevor tried desperately to find a way of proving that he and John were devoted friends, allies in a common cause, comrades in an alien world. He took the only available route.

'He was a jazz fan. He let me have some tapes. Ellington, Lester Young, Beiderbecke, Charlie Parker . . .'

'Charlie Parker!'

Without benefit of sellotape, glaze or compassion, Dawson's

81

face smiled. It was like the sun rising across a hitherto bleak wasteland.

'Charlie Parker!' he repeated.

Trevor knew he had found a fellow freak and therefore all else would follow. Dawson would have given him blood, had that been needed. By the time he left the Registrar's office ten minutes later, he had a promise that all information, county-wide, relating to the deaths of any youngish men called John where there was the possibility of beards and a passion for jazz would be relayed instantly either to San Quentin High or to Jill's house. He would also let Trevor have a tape of Charlie Parker's 1953 concert at Massey Hall in Toronto.

Trevor reported his successes of the morning to Jill in the staffroom at lunchtime, while they ate their fibre sandwiches. They had agreed to avoid the canteen so that their in-depth discussions would not be interrupted by irrelevant wisdom and sexual innuendo from Mr Carter.

Jill was almost impressed by what Trevor had learned about the system of registering births, deaths and marriages.

'How it works is this. If you pop your clogs in hospital, the information goes straight to the big office in town. But this mate of mine, he only picks up the little, informal, local deaths. He's more your cornershop registrar. But he'll try to find out what he can and even better than that . . .'

'There's something better yet to come? I can scarcely believe such a thing.'

'Knock it off,' said Trevor. 'Even better, he's letting me have a tape of Charlie Parker's Massey Hall concert. Bird, Dizzy, Mingus, Bud Powell, Max Roach . . .'

'If it wasn't for total strangers giving you jazz tapes, we wouldn't be involved in all this in the first place.'

'But you want to be involved, 'cos it's about the environment, isn't it?'

Jill had to admit it: she wanted to be involved. Trevor chewed thoughtfully, and a little wearily, on his fibre.

'Mind you,' he said, 'I think the grave-digger was more fun.'

After lunch, Jill left the school by the main door and walked to Trevor's van. As she was failing to unlock the door, Mr Wheeler stepped from his portable shadow.

'Leaving early, Mrs Swinburne?'

'Just popping out on an errand of mercy.'

'Another one?'

'This is the first today. In fact, I'm trying to cut down.'

The headmaster gathered his gown around him and tried to pull himself to his full height, with no perceptible change in his overall dimensions, which remained uncompromisingly weedy.

'Mr Chaplin left the school premises this morning during his free period. He told me that he too was going on an errand of mercy.'

'Different errand. Different brand of mercy,' said Jill, who had no idea what lies Trevor had told Mr Wheeler.

'I understand his errand of mercy was related to the death of an old friend.'

'And mine is to do with showing concern and kindness to the old folk.'

Like a conjurer producing a glass of milk, a brace of rabbits or a gaggle of imperial flags, Jill brandished the bunch of flowers that she had tucked under her arm while failing to unlock the door of Trevor's van.

'Flowers for a sweet old lady who has made her contribution to society and is now a little lonely in the autumn of her years.'

There should have been an angel choir and a large string

section to accompany Jill's smiling concern, but the device worked well enough without artificial aids.

'As I said to Mr Chaplin, blessed are the merciful, for they shall obtain mercy.'

'It's a point of view,' said Jill, as she discovered why she was having trouble unlocking the door of the van. It was already unlocked.

Trevor watched her drive away from the woodwork room. Then he turned to address the assembled class of twelve- and thirteen-year-olds: 'You've probably read in your newspapers about the latest round of education cuts and I've been wondering how to break the news to you about how it'll affect us in woodwork. So I thought I'd just tell you. As from today, you'll all be making one bookend each instead of a pair. You'll find one bookend works perfectly well, used in conjunction with a wall.'

One day just before the First World War, a young girl called Sylvia threw a brick through a window in the cause of women's suffrage. Since then, though a pacifist, she had thrown many objects at many targets, and her aim was good. In the 1930s, she had thrown eggs at Mosleyites, and postwar, rotten tomatoes at rotten cabinet ministers of all parties. She never used fresh fruit or vegetables, because they could be recycled as food for the needy.

When, in 1983, a leading member of the Government had visited the Old Folk's Home to open a new wing, she had organized a demonstration against the same expenditure cuts that were causing Trevor's bookend crisis, and the police had to be called, an unusual happening, even in the moonstruck outer limits of Leeds, where street violence among the over-seventies was rare.

Sylvia was in the grounds of the home, in her wheelchair,

gently demure and grey-haired, eighty-five years old, enjoying the sun, and reading Karl Marx, as Jill approached.

'Sylvia?'

'Jill!'

Sylvia was Jill's guru, as old as the century but, unlike the century, having absorbed the lessons. She was not pleased to see the flowers.

'Flowers?'

'Just to fool the headmaster.'

'We'll give them to that old Tory over there. I'll tell her what to do with them at suppertime. What do you want?'

'I need advice from the oldest suffragette in town.'

'All right. Shall I tell you what *I* need?'

'Tell me.'

'I need to get the hell out of this place. Tell you what. Take me to the park. We'll feed the goddamn ducks.'

Jill pushed the wheelchair across the grass. Sylvia hurled the flowers into the lap of the old Tory. Then they headed due East, towards the park and the ducks and a vision of Jerusalem.

Five

Sylvia was part of Jill Swinburne's life that Trevor knew nothing about. Long before their days of cohabitation, when their relationship comprised lifts to and from school, enlivened by occasional bottles of Frascati and adventures under the duvet, they had discussed, and agreed upon, the importance of personal space and privacy. To be strictly accurate, Jill had discussed it, and Trevor had agreed. His understanding of the arrangement was simple: if he wanted to go to football matches or jazz clubs, he would go alone, or with similarly besotted friends. Meanwhile, she would fill her personal time and space any way that took her fancy. For a time, Trevor suspected this might involve other men, other bottles of Frascati, but the same duvet. This caused him much agony, until he discovered the personal space in question was actually filled by committee meetings and political action, mostly related to saving the environment.

Whenever Jill felt the need to recharge her campaigning batteries, she sought out Sylvia. Like many such friendships, it had started on the Aldermaston road, a road that had doubled for Damascus in many people's lives.

They loved to talk about the great heroines, yes, and about the occasional hero too, of their own and earlier times: trading tales of Red Emma Goldman, Annie Besant, Sylvia Pankhurst, the one member of the family who never deviated and whose name Sylvia herself had inherited. On seeing any hostile element, Sylvia would cry out '*No Pasarán*' – the famous Republican slogan from the Spanish Civil War, coined by a woman, and translated meaning: 'They shall not pass.' They very rarely did. Sylvia was no phoney. She had gone to Spain in the 1930s and had paid her dues.

Her view of the world was clear-cut: people were marvellous and politicians were shit. Asked for evidence she would say: read a history book. In her younger days, when her activities were more public and noisy, and she occasionally went to prison, the newspapers frequently claimed she was in the pay of Moscow.

'Alas,' she said, 'would that it were so.'

She had written to the Kremlin several times, suggesting that they might slip her the odd bar of gold, if only to add substance to the allegations, and ease her later years; nothing ever arrived – not even a nominal kopek. She suspected her mistake was to add a regular PS about sending dissidents to mental institutions.

In accordance with their joint agreement, Jill wheeled Sylvia to the duck pond. She parked the wheelchair beside a low stone wall, where she sat, while listening to some of Sylvia's thoughts on municipal ducks.

'Stupid creatures. They need organizing.'

'And a manifesto?'

'You bet. I've got them all organized at the Home. We have a ten-point programme, starting with the rights of male and female inmates to share rooms if they fancy each other. It's against the rules, can you imagine that? If I fancy some sweet old guy, the rules forbid me to invite him to my bed chamber.'

'You're changing the rules?'

'We're having a civil disobedience campaign. Refusing rice pudding, which is pretty damn sensible if you've ever seen it, and we've blacked all bus trips to the seaside. Why is it that, because you're over seventy, people think you have this rampant lust to go on bus trips to Skegness and Bridlington? I never went before. Why should I go now? I'd rather go dog-racing or boozing.'

'With your sweet old guy?'

Sylvia looked at her, and for the first time that day, the animation and zeal gave way, temporarily, to regret. 'These days I'm only fighting for the principle. Heigh ho and lackaday. What about you, sister? Any sweet guys?'

Jill nodded.

'That's not enough. I want names, descriptions, gory details.'

There are times, thought Jill, when she sounds just like me: I wonder how that happens.

'His name's Trevor Chaplin, he teaches woodwork, and we're living together. Partly because they demolished his flat to make a motorway and he was too idle to find himself another place to live. Partly because . . .'

She hesitated; Sylvia deftly plugged the gap. 'He's a sweet guy?'

'He's a very gentle man.'

'We can all use a little gentility, between revolutions.'

It occurred to Jill that she could make confessions to Sylvia about life with Trevor that she would never make to the man himself – but then, didn't the priesthood operate on the same premise?

Sylvia never liked sentiment to clog the conversation for too long. 'So that's dealt with ducks, sex, old age and love. What did you really want to talk about?'

'Nuclear waste.'

'Easy. We're against it.'

Jill, without thinking, looked around to check for distant watchers, ultra-sonic listening devices and bugged mallards. Sylvia registered her concern.

88

'It's serious?'

She listened carefully to the story so far: the tape recording and how it was delivered; the assorted pursuers, the apparent demise of John the Barman. Listening, the face lost twenty years, and the light of pacifist battle shone brighter.

'A few questions, Sister Swinburne. The people talking on the tapes – are they all men?'

'Yes. Obviously.'

'And do they say where they plan to dump this shit?'

'In one of the Dales.'

Sylvia laughed.

'Is it funny?'

'I only laugh at black jokes. You've got to admit, this is black. Normally, when men start depositing their filth on the planet they pick some place that's already polluted from the last Industrial Revolution. Well away from Whitehall. Hartlepools or Barrow-in-Furness or Glasgow. There's a lot of filth dumped in Scotland. No wonder they hate us.'

She pondered the Dales, and prettiness.

'If they're serious about the Dales, which, as we know, are exceedingly beautiful, part of our island heritage, perfect setting for television commercials, well . . . that is something we can make an issue out of. Where's the tape?'

'In a safe place.'

'Good. And you came to the oldest suffragette in town for guidance?'

'Yes. As ever.'

'Before I give you my considered opinion, I think you should wheel me to another part of the forest.'

Jill was taken by surprise. She was comfortably settled by the water's edge, and quietly enjoying the combination of ancient wisdom and ducks at play.

'Another part of the forest?'

'Wherever you like,' said Sylvia. 'The aviary, the bandstand, the drinking fountain. I want to see whether that man really is watching us.' She glanced at a point in the middle distance, beyond Jill, then continued with her instructions: 'Stand up, without fuss, and wheel me somewhere. You'll see the man I mean. He's standing in the shade of that old apple tree.'

Jill stood up, as instructed, adjusted the blanket covering Sylvia's legs, then moved behind the wheelchair. 'I see him. But it isn't an apple tree.'

'I'm not like you, Jill. All trees look alike to me, apart from poplars. Those are the tall thin ones, aren't they? Poplar trees and apple trees. Those are enough for my world. He is watching us, isn't he?'

'Yes. I know him. He's called Peterson, the man with no name.'

'That's a contradiction, dear.'

'He's the one who claims to break bones.'

'I'd like to meet him.'

As Jill pushed the wheelchair around the pond and towards the tree that was not an apple tree, nor, for that matter, a poplar, she explained something of the Peterson story: his search of her house, his attempts to frighten her and Trevor, and her theory that he represented one of the dirtier limbs of official England.

Sylvia reached a clearcut conclusion. 'Let's give him something to put in his files. They live and die by their files, people like him.'

'Isn't it all on computer these days?'

'The principle holds good, and it stinks.'

Peterson did not move. He realized the two women were heading towards him, and stood his ground. He was not afraid of women or wheelchairs.

'Lovely day for lurking in the park,' said Jill, as they approached Peterson and his sheltering tree.

Peterson said nothing.

'This is my Great-Aunt Sylvia. Great-Aunt Sylvia, this is Mr Peterson, the man with no name, as he's known in the surveillance trade. He breaks bones and he breaks into people's houses.'

'He should be reported to the proper authorities,' said Sylvia in a voice like an irate letter to the *Daily Telegraph*.

'Mrs Swinburne, you've got the story all wrong,' said Peterson, oddly contrite for a man whose image was that of a professional hitman. Sylvia held up a traffic-stopping hand, indicating she wanted her say, and by God, Harry, England, St George and Karl Marx, she was going to have it.

'Young man, you owe us an explanation. I am an old lady, somewhat infirm and therefore invulnerable. You are a young man, fit in wind and limb, therefore also invulnerable. What possible reason do you have for watching me, while lurking in the shade of an old apple tree?'

'It isn't an apple tree, is it?' said Peterson, uncertain of his ability to cope with fearless old ladies, and none too confident about his natural history either: identification of trees had not been part of his training.

'It's nothing to be ashamed of, lurking beneath trees, watching old ladies, provided you have a good reason. Or maybe, being young and strong, you think you can get away with murder. Do you think that, Mr Peterson? Can you get away with murder?'

It was obvious Peterson did not want to be drawn into a discussion about murder.

'Excuse me, I have work to do. Good afternoon, Mrs Swinburne.'

He attempted a smile at Jill, surprisingly. The face was not used to it. The effect was like a thin crack on an icy lake. He did not smile at Sylvia, but turned smartly and walked away from the women in the direction of the main entrance, where the park gates would have been, had they not been taken away during the war. Sylvia and Jill watched him.

'I think we confused him,' said Sylvia.

'But look at the way he walks. He doesn't walk. He marches.'

'To the music of an invisible band.'

They both heard the same music, brassy and martial, with a cannon-like drumbeat and a message to the world that these marchers, whoever they were, would trample over everything in their path. Their ears would hear no other music. It was music to kill and conquer by.

'Take me back to my institution,' said Sylvia.

In an attempt to decontaminate the atmosphere created by the Petersons of the world, they sang on their way back to the Old Folks Home: songs from the Spanish Civil War, songs from Aldermaston, songs from the deep well of the human spirit in revolt against lords and masters. Jill wheeled Sylvia along Elgar Crescent, thrown up – in every sense – during the 1930s by a speculator with a taste for quick profits and the Enigma Variations, in that order. Their voices echoed back from the redbrick semis as they chorused:

> 'We'll make Tony Eden wear a fifty-shilling suit
> When the Red Revolution comes!'

They were stared at by small children, young mothers, elderly dogs, mature joggers and the proprietors of mobile shops, all of them wondering who the hell these women were, and, for that matter, who the hell Tony Eden was. Political analysts were thin on the ground in Elgar Crescent, especially in the middle of the afternoon.

In between songs, Sylvia and Jill discussed the best course

of action, given a clandestine tape recording concerned with nuclear waste.

On her return to school, Jill had one period of English to teach. Her closing words to the class were; 'For your homework, I'd like those of you who have copies of *A Midsummer Night's Dream* to read Act One and then in our next lesson you can tell those who do not have copies what the story is so far.'

At the same moment, in the woodwork room, Trevor's closing words to his class were: 'For your homework, I want all of you to have a good look at your dining room table when you get home, and next lesson you can tell me how the legs are fastened to the top.'

'How will you mark it, sir?' asked a sharp youth called Tennyson.

'Very quickly and very easily,' said Trevor, marking down Tennyson as a lad to watch and, if necessary, quell.

In the staffroom, Jill and Trevor agreed on the difficulties of teaching English and woodwork without books or wood.

Mr Carter complained about the difficulties of scrambling through his day without the company of his favourite colleagues.

'Mr Chaplin, Mrs Swinburne, you would not believe the loneliness of my existence when, each time I crave your presence, I look from the window, and you are leaving the school premises.'

'We've had a lot of errands of mercy today,' said Trevor.

'Both of you? Errands of mercy?'

He sniffed the possibility of misery, since the word mercy implied somebody, somewhere, in trouble.

'I took an old lady to the park and we didn't feed the ducks,' said Jill.

'That's a bit mean,' said Trevor.

'The ducks are fatter than us.'

'Was this a real old lady?' asked Mr Carter.

'Yes. Complete with a wheelchair.'

'A real errand of mercy. I naturally assumed you were lying. Was yours a real errand of mercy, Mr Chaplin?'

Trevor shrugged.

'Sort of yes and sort of no. It was more to do with Charlie Parker and gravediggers.'

This reassured Mr Carter, because it sounded untrue; he was happiest with half-truths, deception and innuendo. It confirmed his view of the world as a conglomeration of confusion.

'Come on,' said Jill to Trevor, tapping him on the shoulder.

'I know I'm supposed to know where we're going but I've forgotten.'

'The third thing. We're going to the supermarket.'

'Sorry. I'd forgotten.'

Mr Carter's face lit up, like the Eddystone lighthouse with the aid of a new wick.

'You two are going to the supermarket? Together?'

'Yes,' said Jill. 'I think that's what I just said. We are going to the supermarket.'

'I drive the van. Mrs Swinburne does the heavy lifting.'

'But don't you realize, my dear friends, you have confirmed what I'd always suspected?'

'We don't even know what you're talking about,' said Jill.

'This thing you two are doing. Cohabitation. Is that the word?'

'It depends what you're talking about,' said Jill, taking seven assorted plastic carrier bags from her locker.

In an unusual show of intimacy, Mr Carter put his arms around Jill and Trevor, both of whom winced at the gesture.

'I am talking about living together in what my mother

94

used to call sin. Cohabitation. And I am right. To the naked eye, it is practically indistinguishable from marriage.'

The cohabs freed themselves from his tentative embrace and aimed for the door by the shortest route.

'Under no circumstances buy the special offer chili con carne,' Mr Carter shouted across the room. 'It makes the entire galaxy erupt.'

Trevor and Jill were within touching distance of the van when Mr Wheeler loomed from behind the bonnet of a BMW, property of a young PE teacher, who supplemented his income by working as a disc jockey and, according to Three B, as a male stripper, under the name of Sid Adonis.

'Another errand of mercy, Mr Chaplin, Mrs Swinburne?'

'It's four o'clock, we're going home,' said Trevor, who was sick of cross-examinations about his private life.

'While I have the two of you on the premises, may I remind you about four o'clock tomorrow?'

'Four o'clock tomorrow?' asked Jill, with the calculated uncertainty of one who wanted to give the impression that she really knew all about four o'clock tomorrow but would welcome a nudge about the room number. The headmaster took the hint and made his formal announcement, not difficult for a man who normally conversed in formal announcements.

'There will be a meeting in the hall at four o'clock tomorrow to discuss the school trip to Holland, which the three of us are leading. I trust you hadn't forgotten *that*.'

They hadn't forgotten that. It was like asking Ann Boleyn whether she had forgotten the jolly wheezes planned for after breakfast.

'We are counting the days with eager anticipation,' said Jill.

Driving to the supermarket, Trevor said, 'I've been thinking about the Holland trip.'

'What about it?'

95

'I don't want to go.'

In the still small period of time since moving in with Jill, Trevor Chaplin had discovered that there was much more to cohabitation than finding somewhere to dump the records. Each small crevice of his being was subjected to intense scrutiny and assessment. Supermarket shopping was a typical example.

When he lived in his attic, he called at the supermarket once a week for butter, sugar, eggs, bacon and beans. He kept the eggs, bacon and beans in reserve for those occasions, like Christmas, when the takeaway was closed, or for when it was raining, or when his system was vindalooed into indifference.

One evening, after the supermarket had closed, he had visited a conventional, old-fashioned grocery shop, of the kind that occasionally breeds prime ministers, because Jill was coming to the flat and he needed some butter. The grocer had asked him, 'New Zealand or Danish?' Unaware of the issues involved in such a decision, he had replied, 'Yellow.' Later that same evening, he discovered Jill never ate butter anyway; she preferred margarine, because – as far as he could recall – it was less cruel to whales.

Pushing the trolley along the aisles of the supermarket, he always counted ten before suggesting any item for purchase. Flanked by toiletries, some of which puzzled him, he plucked up courage.

'Suntan oil? For our holiday?'

'In Holland? We're more likely to get rusty.'

Wheeling his way into the fresh fruit and vegetables, he felt a little more secure. Most of the items grew in the soil and he knew that Jill thought highly of soil.

'Grapefruit. They're good for you, aren't they?'

He was so confident that he took two grapefruit from the shelf, and placed them carefully in the trolley.

'Put them back,' snapped Jill.

Trevor put them back at once, then asked, 'Why?'

'We don't buy anything South African.'

'Sorry.'

He remembered.

The idea was simple enough: any government that treated people like dirt should be punished by having its consumer items ignored in the supermarket. Jill had explained some of the rises and falls in this department. South Africa was a permanent fall. Spain, Portugal and Greece had been falls, but were now rises. South America and the Middle East were too complicated to explain to Trevor. He had absorbed rule number one: South African goods were out and he was content to leave it at that. Indeed, he was one of the few people who related the apartheid problem to jazz. His preferred music was, at root, a black African music, and any government that persecuted black people was, simultaneously, persecuting Duke Ellington, Charlie Parker and Miles Davis. Q.E.D.

Practically every item on every supermarket shelf was scrutinized in this way. Pushing the trolley into the tinned fruit section he thought, we'll have problems here.

'Used to love pineapple chunks when I was little.'

'Help yourself,' said Jill.

He reached out for a tin.

'Not those, Trevor, put them back.'

'Pardon?'

'Read what it says on the tin.'

He did as he was told. 'Finest selected pineapple pieces in syrup.'

'Precisely.'

'I'm sorry. I can't see anything wrong in that.'

97

'We only buy tinned fruit in its own juice. Read the small print, you'll also find the syrup contains chemical artificial sweetener.'

Trevor read the small print, as instructed. Jill was right. He put the tin back on the shelf. Memories of their previous trip to the supermarket came into his mind: artificial sweeteners were wicked, as were chemical additives and colouring agents. He was not sure whether they came from fascist countries or caused heart attacks or both, though he was fairly confident that blue whales were not involved.

It was a relief to move into the one area where he was totally confident: unit pricing.

Jill was constantly complaining about the manufacturers' habit of putting their wares in packets of many and diverse shapes and sizes. She picked up two such packages.

'How is anybody supposed to choose between these two? This one costs thirty-one pence for two hundred and fifty grams. The other one costs thirty-seven pence for three hundred grams. How are we supposed to tell which is the better value?'

'Easy,' said Trevor. 'Buy the second one.'

'Are you sure?'

'Yes. You get eight-point-one grams for your penny as against eight-point-nought-six with the other.'

'You worked that out in your head?'

'Yes. I'm not just a plain face, you know.'

Trevor's ability in unit pricing generally won him a kiss in the closing stages of the supermarket expedition.

'You're amazing at unit pricing, did you know that?'

'Used to call it mental arithmetic when I was little. I think it was eating all those pineapple chunks in syrup.'

'Knock it off, smartarse.'

Trevor's hard-won moral advantage, gained by his mental arithmetic, evaporated with the toilet rolls. Jill asked him to reach for them from a high shelf and as he put them in the trolley, he sensed her disapproval, so much so that the two of them said in unison, 'Put them back, Trevor.'

'Why?' he asked.

'They're pink.'

I've unit priced the lot. With these you get two hundred and eighty sheets and with the others you get . . .'

'They're pink!'

'I know they're pink.'

'What did I tell you about pink toilet rolls?'

He tried very hard to remember what Jill had told him about pink toilet rolls. He remembered the conversation, in this same section of the supermarket, but it was towards the end of their shopping, and his brain had seized up. He had retreated into his head, and was replaying Lionel Hampton's solo on the 1947 recording of 'Star Dust' at the time of her lecture. He tried guesswork.

'Pink toilet rolls contain artificial chemical syrup manufactured in Cape Town?'

'They are non-biodegradeable.'

'I was close.'

He traded the pink toilet rolls for white ones and edged the trolley, hope in his heart, towards the check-out counter. In the queue, he tried the puckish smile which had, regularly during their life together, won handsome dividends, ofttimes erotic.

'Have I been really good? Have I saved us lots of money with my amazing skill at unit pricing?'

'What do you want?'

'Bag of toffees?'

Close to the check-out tills were displays of chocolate, sweets and potato crisps, carefully placed to extract the final fragments of copper coin from the weary consumer.

'It's entirely up to you, Trevor.'

He took a small packet of toffees from the rack.

'What happens to your teeth is your business.'

He put the toffees back. Her reference to teeth concealed a longer-term threat. She had several times murmured a phrase that he dreaded: 'dental appointment'. On the one occasion the subject had been properly aired, the exchange had run: 'When did you last have a dental check?'

'About a year ago.'

If Trevor had told the whole truth and nothing but the truth, his answer would have been, 'August 1977, but I didn't turn up.' There were many fears and traumas buried in the act of replacing a bag of toffees.

Driving out of the supermarket car park, Jill asked him to make a detour by way of the Post Office.

'Why?'

'I want to post something.'

'There's no better place.'

The Post Office was a small, amiable shambles of a shop that also sold second-hand typewriters, greetings cards, old paperbacks and an occasional frying pan. People gathered there in large numbers to cash their meagre state benefits and talk to each other. It was due to close in three months' time, in the cause of greater efficiency, and Jill had started a petition intended to make officialdom consider human factors, accepting that such thinking might create a precedent in high places. It was an old-fashioned Post Office, on a street, and you could park anything outside: bicycles, dogs, cars or yellow vans.

Jill gave Trevor a small package.

'Post that for me, and you can have a treat.'

He took the package, which was already stamped, and dropped it in the postbox.

He climbed back into the van.

'That thing I posted. It felt like a tape.'

'Yes,' said Jill.

'Was it a tape?'

'Yes.'

'Is that all you're going to tell me?'

'Yes.'

'What about my treat? You said if I posted your package I could have a treat.'

'A pizza.'

'Whyebuggerman!'

Two hundred yards along the High Street from the Post Office was the Giaconda Pizza Palace, housed in premises that had once been the local Co-op. When co-operation hit bad times, the building decayed for a few years, before two middle-aged men invested their redundancy money in what they perceived to be a trend in the moonstruck outer limits of Leeds: pizzas, pasta, Neopolitan muzak and plastic foliage. They painted the walls in primary colours, bought some bentwood chairs, hired some noisy Italian waiters from Wakefield and stayed open all hours. Jill disapproved of the place on every possible basis: political, ideological, dietary and aesthetic. Trouble was, she enjoyed eating there.

They placed their orders: a jumbo-sized John Charles pizza for Trevor, a small Geoffrey Boycott vegetarian lasagne for Jill. All the dishes were named after local sporting heroes. The wine list offered a choice between house red and house white. Every autumn it was supplemented by Beaujolais Nouveau, and Trevor had once caused a stir by asking the waiter what year it was.

Over their John Charles, Geoffrey Boycott and house white, Jill gave Trevor edited highlights of her meeting in the park, without revealing any of her innermost feelings of tenderness towards him, feelings that she had felt safe in sharing with Sylvia.

'I have been advised,' she said, a little pompously as the

house white took effect, 'that at all times we should try to confuse the enemy.'

'Good,' said Trevor. 'What does that mean?'

'It means . . . confuse the enemy.'

'Will it confuse the enemy if I have some pudding?'

'Go on,' she said, sliding the menu across the table, 'and I promise not to mention teeth.'

The enemy was waiting when they returned home. Jill was first into the living room, carrying a box of groceries. Trevor was following with the seven plastic carriers when she dropped the box.

Peterson was standing in the room, in front of where the fireplace would have been, had there been a fireplace. Trevor put the plastic carrier bags on the settee to pick up Jill's box.

'You can frighten people, doing this, you know,' he said to Peterson.

'That, Mr Chaplin, Mrs Swinburne, is the object of the exercise.'

Six

Dropping the groceries on the living room floor released the tension from Jill; she no longer felt frightened of Peterson, though she retained a grudging respect for his ability to break into houses, undetected and without damaging the property.

'Mr Peterson,' she announced, 'is this going to be highly melodramatic, or may we pack away the groceries before you start giving lectures about national security? I assume it is national security?'

'It is.'

Trevor picked up the cue from Jill. 'Thing is, we'd like to get the frozen stuff into the fridge before it thaws. It's like that old hymn.'

'What old hymn?' said Jill. 'You don't know any old hymns.'

'Rescue the perishables.'

Peterson nodded agreement. The precise movement of the head was no more than a millimetre. He had a minimalist approach to smiling and head-nodding. Jill and Trevor stored away the supermarket shopping in strict accordance with the Swinburne system of food storage, a unique combination of logic and mysticism. Trevor concentrated on those disciplines where he felt most confident: putting vegetables in the rack, bread in the breadbin and water in the kettle.

'Would you like a cup of tea, Mr Peterson? We generally have one when we've been shopping.'

Peterson nodded again, all of two millimetres this time. Obviously he was a tea junky.

'Milk and sugar,' he said.

'No sugar,' said Jill, reprovingly. 'We discourage sugar. We can offer you a sweetening tablet, though it's important to warn you that they can be addictive.'

Wincing as he sipped his unsweetened tea, Peterson addressed them with cool severity. Trevor and Jill sat side by side on the settee. Peterson remained standing. He was happiest standing, preferably to attention, though he punctuated this with moments of disciplined pacing and heel-clicking. His shoes shone brightly, like two black Volkswagens parked next to each other.

'You are quite right, Mrs Swinburne. We have to talk about national security.'

'What about *our* security?' said Jill. 'This is the second time you've broken into our house, to our knowledge.'

'Only because national security is involved.'

Peterson set off on a short route-march, the length of the non-existent fireplace, before resuming his guardsman's stance, protecting the standard lamp against unnamed foreign powers.

'Let's not mess about. We know all about you two. We know, for example, that Mr Chaplin went to the cemetery this morning, and from there he went to the registrar's office in Waterhouse Street. We also know that Mrs Swinburne went to the Old Folks Home, from there she took an old lady in the park, then returned to school. We know that after school, you both went to the supermarket, and from there to the Giaconda Pizza Palace.'

'We stopped at the Post Office on the way,' said Trevor.

'Don't worry. We know about the Post Office.'

'What's the big deal?' asked Jill. 'We know about these things too.'

'Put all these things together, and they make a pattern. All these comings and goings, all these meetings . . . they're all related to one thing. The tape.'

'You're still on about that tape?' said Jill.

'More tea?' said Trevor.

Peterson shook his head. 'Where is the tape, Mrs Swinburne?'

'I told you. It's in the canal.'

'We even showed you the canal,' added Trevor.

'I said we knew about you two. You may be surprised how much we know.'

'I'll have some more tea,' said Jill.

Trevor took Jill's beaker, a politically motivated item bearing the word 'Peace' in twenty-three languages, and his own, which proclaimed unswerving allegiance to Sunderland FC, and poured more tea.

'We know, Mrs Swinburne, that you have a long record as a political subversive. We know, Mr Chaplin, that you are a long-term associate of Mrs Swinburne's.'

'I'm not an associate, I'm a cohab.'

'We know, in addition, about the events of last year.'

'Last year? What happened last year?' Jill said, turning to Trevor.

'Everton won the League. Cootie Williams died. Three B set fire to the cycle shed.'

Peterson was looking for none of these answers. 'You two involved yourselves in a situation that culminated in a senior police officer having to leave the force and a local councillor and a businessman going to prison.'

'I believe a local branch of the Freemasons had to close down permanently,' Jill said, then regretted it.

'Exactly!' Peterson clicked his heels.

'Exactly what?' said Trevor, aware that the whole business outlined by the man with no name had been his fault in the beginning: when his need for a set of special-offer Bix Beiderbecke records had drawn them into close contact with the local black economy, masterminded by the ubiquitous Big Al and his friend and occasional brother, Little Norm. For reasons Trevor had not yet fathomed, his musical quest had culminated in the exposure of major corruption in high places.

'Exactly this,' said Peterson. 'Mrs Swinburne is the sort of person who, presented with a challenge, refuses to look the other way. She tells me she threw the tape into the canal. I do not believe her. She is a self-confessed radical. We know what was on the tape. We know she would not throw it into the canal. We know she would do other things with it.'

'Stop talking about me as if I wasn't here! Anybody would think I was physically handicapped.'

'What have you done with the tape, Mrs Swinburne?'

'You know everything. You tell me, Mr Peterson.'

'Very well. I will tell you.'

Peterson slipped his hand into his pocket, and brought out a package.

'You called at the Post Office on your way from the supermarket to the Giaconda Pizza Palace. You posted this.' He held up the package for their inspection, like a conjuror inviting an audience to confirm that his hands are firmly attached to his arms. 'This is your package?'

'Of course it is. Trevor posted it for me.'

'And what's inside?'

'It's personal. None of your business.'

'Is it a tape?'

'I repeat. It's personal and none of your business.'

'May I ask a question?' said Trevor, feeling a bit left out.

'Ask your question, Mr Chaplin.'

'I posted that a couple of hours ago. How did you get it? Either you've got very thin arms or you've got influence.'

106

Peterson smiled, arctically. 'Wheels within wheels, Mr Chaplin.'

The wheels of Dawson's bicycle creaked a little, as he pedalled up the long hill leading from the cement canyons of the Clement Attlee housing estate to the executive suburbs where the mortgagees lived. He had set off energetically, with Charlie Parker's 'Billie's Bounce' in his head, setting the tempo for his legs. Now Johnny Hodges was playing 'Jeep's Blues'. It was a very slow blues, but Dawson's legs were short and the hill was long.

Peterson scrutinized the package, as a scientist might examine a blood sample giving the ultimate clue to the problem of premature baldness.

'This package is addressed to a Mr J. Harrison of Chorlton-cum-Hardy. Who is he?'

'He's my Uncle Jack,' said Jill, 'and you'll never guess where he lives.'

'And why are you sending him a tape?'

'Promise you won't break any of my bones, Mr Peterson, but I am sending Uncle Jack a tape because he likes George Formby.'

'George Formby?'

Peterson was neither amused nor impressed. He tore open the package, which was several layers deep in brown paper and Sellotape, with strength and controlled venom.

Deep within the package he discovered a tape.

'It doesn't have George Formby written on it.' He passed it round for inspection.

'You should always identify your tapes, otherwise your files get in a terrible mess,' said Trevor.

'I forgot,' said Jill.

It was Trevor's turn to scrutinize the tape. 'I'll tell you one thing for nothing. This tape's never been anywhere near a canal.'

'Play it!' barked Peterson.

'Do you like George Formby?' asked Jill.

'You know as well as I do, Mrs Swinburne, that that tape has nothing to do with George Formby. Play it, Mr Chaplin!'

'Play that thing,' Trevor murmured to himself, as he crossed to the stereo unit, adding a little more loudly, 'Side A or Side B?'

'Just play it!'

Trevor loaded the tape into the cassette holder and pressed the 'Play' button. There was a pause, followed by a hiss, followed by some incoherent clicks, followed by a cheerful, nasal Lancastrian singing that he was leaning on the lamppost at the corner of the street in case a certain little lady passed by.

Peterson was not to be fooled. He crossed to the stereo unit, pressed the 'Stop' button, then wound the tape forward, before pressing the 'Play' button again. The same cheerful voice sang about the sights you see when you're cleaning windows.

Peterson continued his stop-start exploration of the tape. He listened, with Trevor and Jill, to fragments of songs embracing every cosmic issue from flannelette nightshirts to little sticks of Blackpool rock.

'Funny how George Formby's still popular even after all these years,' said Jill.

'These things go in cycles,' said Trevor.

Dawson was cycling along a level stretch of road. In the full bloom of youth he might have pedalled to the up-tempo pulse of Woody Herman's 'Caldonia', but as befits a man of one score year and ten, he settled into the more comfortable medium bounce of Benny Goodman's 'Don't Be That Way' from the 1938 Carnegie Hall concert.

Peterson removed the tape from the stereo deck. 'I accept the truth of what you say, Mrs Swinburne. This is unquestionably George Formby.' He returned the tape to Jill.

'That's very decent of you,' she said, 'bearing in mind it is the truth.'

'But I do not accept for one minute that the tape I am looking for is in the Blackwater Canal.' He crossed to the door. 'I may well be back.'

'If we're not here, just let yourself in,' said Trevor.

Peterson had parked his long, black saloon car discreetly round a corner. By instinct and training, he always tried to park out of sight from the entire human race. As he was reversing out of the executive cul-de-sac, he felt a slight bump on the side of the car. Looking out of the window he saw Dawson and his bicycle sprawled in an apparently uninjured heap on the grass verge. He climbed out of the car.

'Are you all right?'

Dawson straightened up into a sitting position, doing a swift count of his primary limbs and accessories.

'Bearing in mind I just fell off my bike, not bad at all, considering.'

A plastic carrier bag bearing the name 'Mole Jazz' lay on the grass beside the bicycle. Peterson picked up Dawson, the bicycle and the carrier bag, in that order. By instinct and training, he always investigated other people's property. In the carrier bag he saw half a dozen tapes.

'Tapes?'

'Yes.'

Peterson smiled, this time with a genuine show of teeth. 'On your way to see Mr Chaplin and Mrs Swinburne by any chance?'

'Mr Chaplin, yes . . .'

'What a happy little coincidence!' said Peterson, slipping the tapes into his pocket.

Dawson protested, but was quietened by a short lecture on the theory and practice of bone-breaking in the second half of the twentieth century.

Jill and Trevor agreed that while they were delighted to be rid of Peterson, they had not been impressed by his performance. Here was a man who claimed founder membership of the National Union of Hit-Men and Bone-Breakers and the most violent actions of the whole evening had been the tearing open of a package, and the angry pressing of a 'Rewind' button.

'On the other hand,' said Jill, 'he apparently has the power to steal mail from the Post Office.'

'Isn't that against the law?'

'I think our Mr Peterson *is* the law. They're probably listening to our phone calls as well.'

'Are you telling me he's special branch or MI something?'

'I should think so.'

Like supermarket shopping, their attitudes to law and order reflected divergent views of the Universe. As a long-time campaigner, demonstrator and marcher, Jill liked to think that her phone was bugged, her mail was opened and her life under more or less permanent surveillance by those whom she wished to destroy, or drive mad, in either order. As a long-time non-campaigner and passionate abstainer, Trevor was content to let the great and the good pursue their tacky ways, providing they left him alone to listen to his music, pore over the football results and teach a little wood-work on the side.

Jill was flattered that MI something-or-other was taking an interest in her activities. Trevor was nervous and in no way reassured when the doorbell rang.

'He's come back to break some bones.'

'Don't be a baby. I'll go.'

Jill answered the door, and returned, to Trevor's relief, with Dawson, looking rather more bedraggled than he had when sitting behind his desk at the Registrar's office that morning.

'Mr Dawson says he's a friend of yours.'

'Hello,' said Trevor. 'Yes, he works for the Registrar of Births, Deaths and Marriages.'

'Waterhouse Street branch,' added Dawson, with a regis-trar's concern for full and accurate reportage. 'And you must be Mrs Chaplin?'

'No. In your terms I am Mrs Swinburne. In my terms I am Ms Swinburne. If you're a friend of Trevor's, I suppose I must be Jill. But in no sense am I Mrs Chaplin. Nor is he Mr Swinburne.'

'To tell you the truth, I'm not sure whether I'm a friend of Mr Chaplin's or not.'

'Of course you're a friend. You're a Charlie Parker fan and you're bringing me some tapes.'

'Well, I did *try* to bring you some tapes. May I sit down? I fell off my bike and I feel a little woozy.'

Jill eased Dawson gently into the nearest armchair. She gave Trevor a look that said, I'm sure there's a reasonable and sensible explanation, but please let it be brief.

'How do you mean, you did try?' asked Trevor.

'I tried to bring you some tapes. Charlie Parker, Dizzy Gillespie, Bud Powell, Thelonius Monk . . . but a man took them off me.' His face was that of a little boy deprived of a toffee apple by a bigger boy.

'A man took them off you?' Trevor had a theory congealing in his mind as to the identity of the man.

'He knocked me off my bike just around the corner from here. He was in this big black car with smoked glass windows and he saw the tapes in the carrier bag and said I bet those are for Mr Chaplin and I said yes and he took them off me and when I tried to get them back he said he'd break my arms and legs.'

Dawson's explanation used almost as much breath as the bicycle ride from his home, and he had to rest for a few minutes.

'That would be Mr Peterson. We call him the man with no name.' Dawson nodded, without understanding, as Jill continued to explain, 'He's a kind of friendly, neighbourhood special branch. A community spy. Searches the house, bugs the phone and follows us everywhere we go.'

'Is he into jazz?'

'I very much doubt it,' said Jill. 'I imagine he's more for military bands and Wagner.'

'Are you feeling better now?' asked Trevor.

'A bit.'

Dawson's face, battleship grey on his arrival, had now resumed its normal translucent pink.

'And how's your bike?'

'Bent. Only somewhat. Not badly. If I can leave it here overnight, I'll get a bus home.'

'You'll do nothing of the sort. I'll give you a lift. You ride halfway across the county bringing me tapes and get knocked off your bike by a man with no name . . . it's the least I can do to give you a lift home.'

'I didn't actually bring you any tapes.'

'But you did try,' said Jill.

112

Dawson stood up. 'And on the way home I'll tell you about the funeral.'

'Funeral?'

'Funeral?'

On the way home to the concrete sanctuary of the Clement Attlee estate, Dawson explained to Trevor about the funeral.

'After you called this morning, I phoned a mate at head office. You'd like him, he's into Kansas City music . . . Count Basie, Benny Moten, the Blue Devils . . .'

'Great.'

'I told him what you'd told me . . . a recent death . . . bloke with beard who worked in a pub . . . a Beiderbecke fan . . . and he said he'd call back if he heard anything. Couple of hours later he called back.'

'With a death?'

'He'd rung around the branches . . . came back with this.' Dawson produced a piece of paper from his pocket. 'From our Barstow Street branch. Tomorrow there's a funeral. Name . . . John Stringfellow . . . killed in a car crash . . . aged forty-one. My mate thinks he used to go to that jazz club, Birdland.'

'Birdland in New York?'

Dawson shook his head.

'No. In Hunslet. They used to meet in the back room of the the Flying Ferret. It only lasted a month. The landlord threw them out. Seems he was into Gregorian chant. But your man used to go there. Beard, duffel coat, CND badge. If that's your man.'

'It sounds like him.'

'Well, there you are.'

He put the slip of paper on the dashboard, with the

old soccer programmes, unpaid parking tickets, and toffee wrappers of a lost era.

'And the funeral's tomorrow?'

'Half-past four,' said Dawson, adding as an afterthought, 'At the cemetery.'

'Sounds like the ideal place.'

In bed, Jill Swinburne and Trevor were experimenting. In a search for deeper, mutual understanding they were reading each other's books. Jill was reading *Beneath the Underdog* by Charles Mingus. Trevor was reading *The Female Eunuch* by Germaine Greer. They had both found rude bits and concluded they had more in common than originally suspected.

They also discussed funerals.

'You can't just turn up at a complete stranger's funeral,' said Jill.

'Yes you can. I've been going to family funerals all my life and they're always full of strangers.'

'All right. You go.'

'Me? On my own?'

'Trevor, we did agree. You would investigate the death of John the barman. I would work out an overall strategy with Sylvia at the Old People's Home. Death is your department.'

'Thanks.'

He lay in silence for a while, wondering whether to ask the precise meaning of three of the words in the book, then changed his mind. He closed the book and climbed out of bed.

'Where are you going?'

'Here.'

He stood beside the dresser and pulled open the drawer that Jill allocated to him for his smaller garments.

'What are you doing?'

'This.'

He pulled out various items of clothing one at a time, while mumbling a short soliloquy to himself: 'Excuse me, you don't know me, I am a long-lost cousin or friend of the deceased, except I'm not absolutely sure I'm at the right funeral, could you let me have a detailed description of the late Mr Stringfellow, better still, maybe you could just lift the lid for a moment and . . .'

'Trevor!'

'Well, it's daft, isn't it? What if it is John the barman? What's it got to do with tapes about nuclear waste? And will I end up with my bones broken? Or in the canal? And where is the bloody tape anyway?'

'In a safe place.'

Trevor pounced on something in the drawer.

'Got it!' he said, triumphantly.

'Got what?'

He held up a black tie. 'I shall need it if I'm going to a funeral tomorrow.'

In the early 1960s, property developers and financiers prowled the North of England, brandishing bags of gold before the eyes of councils, great and small, making an offer that few could refuse: allow us to demolish your town centre, your much-loved but obsolescent market halls and High Streets, your ancient tea-houses and variety theatres, your bakeries and butcheries, your tie shops and pie shops, and we will give you in return mighty skyscrapers and crystal palaces, precincts and parking lots and a nominal mural or piece of sculpture and the people will rise in their thousands and cry: verily, this is the Athens of the North.

The gold changed hands, the old towns were demolished and still there was only one Athens in the world, where it had always been, in Greece. The North of England was left with an abundance of office blocks, unwanted, unloved, unused. Signs were put up saying, GUARD DOGS, but nobody ever saw a dog.

In the outer moonstruck limits of Leeds were many such buildings. Some of them glowed in the dark like dying television screens.

Redundant skyscrapers are a major asset to people who, for professional purposes, wish to remain decently reticent about the murky way they make their living. Peterson was such a man, not that he regarded his calling as murky: rather as a missionary crusade against the forces of evil in our midst. He could spot an enemy within at a thousand paces.

While Trevor was looking for his black tie, Peterson was buried deep in a glass skyscraper, sitting at a desk in a windowless room – a tricky commodity to come by in a glass box – playing tapes. He heard the dazzling torrents of Charlie Parker; the glistering pyrotechnics of Dizzy Gillespie; the sad, spiky arpeggios of Bud Powell; the quirky harmonies of Thelonius Monk, the piano player with limping fingers and whose middle name was Sphere; and he hated them all, with a furious passion. He was not in the market for music. Poets are not right all the time, because the more music that Peterson heard, the more savage became his breast.

Next day, Trevor Chaplin took a suitcase to school. As he and Jill were leaving the van, Yvonne Fairweather called out cheerfully, 'Going on your holidays, sir?'

'Life is one long holiday, my dear,' he replied.

As he walked into the staffroom, Mr Carter looked at him, over the top of page three of somebody else's newspaper.

'Going on your holidays, Mr Chaplin?'

'No, I'm selling brushes, door to door. And the next person

116

that asks me if I'm going on my holidays gets a kick up the bum.'

As he walked into his woodwork room, Mr Wheeler was lying in wait.

'Ah! Are you going on your holidays, Mr Chaplin?'

'Er . . . no . . . I'm . . . not going on my holidays, Mr Wheeler.'

'In point of fact you *are* going on your holidays, but not today. School trip. Don't forget. Meeting in the hall at four o'clock to discuss the arrangements.'

The headmaster did not wait for a reply. He did not regard meetings in the hall as negotiable. Trevor replied after Mr Wheeler had left the room.

'No, I hadn't forgotten the meeting, you lunkhead. I'm just not coming, that's all.'

Trevor locked the suitcase in a cupboard before anybody could ask any more questions about his holidays. It would not be needed until the end of the afternoon.

At four o'clock, Mr Wheeler faced an assortment of young people in the hall, about forty in all, including Yvonne Fairweather and her highly personal branch of the Cosa Nostra, all of whom had decided a school trip to Holland with Mrs Swinburne and Mr Chaplin would be good fun. Jill, sitting at a safe distance, wondered at their judgement, and her own.

The headmaster fluttered his academic gown and addressed the multitude.

'If Mr Chaplin were here we could start. He is coming, Mrs Swinburne, as far as we are aware?'

'As far as we are aware, yes, Mr Wheeler. Why don't you start and I will pass your wisdom on to him at a later stage?'

'Very well.'

He realized her suggestion made total sense, but resented the fact that it was not his idea. He unrolled a map on an easel set to one side of the stage, where the grand piano would stand when the school had raised enough money to buy one. The piano fund currently stood at £17.58, enough, as Mr Carter loved to point out, to buy a scale in the key of C, but strictly no black notes.

The map duly unrolled and exhibited, Mr Wheeler turned to the students.

'Can anybody tell me what this is?'

'A map, sir,' said Yvonne.

'A map of where?'

'Even money says it's Holland.'

'I beg your pardon?'

'Holland, sir,' said Yvonne brightly.

'Holland indeed.'

He paced slowly up and down the stage, like a caged sloth.

'I have always found that any holiday is best appreciated if it is preceded by a careful study of the geography, history and culture of the place one is about to visit.'

His observations on the nature of holidays were marred by the clump of footsteps. He paused to see Trevor walking down the aisle, wearing dark suit, white shirt, black tie and black shoes. He had not worn the black shoes since he was best man at his brother's wedding, and he had forgotten they clumped.

Trevor arrived at the foot of the stage, and he and the headmaster both waited until the echoes of the clumping died away.

'Sorry I'm late, Mr Wheeler, but I had to get changed. As you can see.'

'I noticed the difference.'

Trevor was famous for his normal everyday wear: jeans, check shirt and lumberjacket. He looked like a man who had come to fix the plumbing but as he pointed out to anybody who challenged him on the subject, you don't wear a tuxedo if you teach woodwork because the bow tie gets clogged up with sawdust. Mr Wheeler certainly noticed the difference.

'I assume there is a reason for the suit and the black tie?'

'Yes. I have to go to a funeral.'

'After the meeting?'

'No, I'm afraid not. I have to go, more or less now. It's . . .' He hesitated, then flung in the old favourite: '. . . an errand of mercy.'

'What time is this funeral?'

'Four-thirty. Prompt.'

Not the most sensitive of men, Mr Wheeler knew a barrel when he was over it. He sighed a deep sigh that implied his dislike of Trevor and all those members of staff who conspired daily to subvert his vision of his school as it might be, which, for all practical purposes, meant every teacher in the school.

'Very well, Mr Chaplin. Perhaps Mrs Swinburne will report to you on the essential items of my talk?'

'I'm sure she will.'

Aware of the need to set a good example to the assembly, all of whom were giggling at Trevor's suit, Mr Wheeler added, 'And my condolences.'

'Thank you. It's a difficult time for everybody, but . . .'

He allowed his voice to peter out in what he hoped was a reasonable show of controlled emotion. He tried to leave the hall quietly. The more resolutely he tiptoed, the louder the clumps. As he left the hall, he heard Mr Wheeler raising his voice above the noise of his shoes and the laughter of Yvonne Fairweather's mob: 'I have always found that any holiday is best appreciated . . .'

Trevor parked his van outside the cemetery, then went in by the main gate. At the far end of a long gravel path he could see a group of mourners gathered round a grave. He walked along the path. Instead of clumping, he crunched. It made a change, of sorts.

A voice called to him, quietly, from the shelter of a tree to one side of the path.

'Mr Chaplin, isn't it?'

He stopped, turned, and saw John the barman.

'Yes, it's Mr Chaplin. It's . . . er . . . John the barman, isn't it? From the Hay Wain?'

'Glad you remembered.'

'Whyebuggerman.'

John seemed a little surprised by Trevor's choice of words, and by his choice of clothes; even on a brief acquaintanceship, he had Trevor marked down as man who dressed like a seaside boarding-house bed, late in the season.

'Are you here for somebody's funeral?'

'Yes,' said Trevor. 'Yours.'

They stared at each other, looking for a way out of several interlocking dilemmas and contradictions.

Eventually, John said, 'Let's both go.'

They walked along the path towards the open grave.

Seven

It was obvious to Trevor Chaplin and John the barman, from the moment they met in the cemetery, that the funeral was somebody else's; but it made sense to double-check.

They hung around the fringes of the ceremony at the graveside, catching occasional words from the minister. He would never win prizes for volume, projection or clarity, but one phrase reached the extremities of the gathering: 'Our dear departed sister Hannah.'

'Do you know anybody called Hannah?' asked John.

'Shhh!' hissed a bystander.

Once everybody's sister Hannah had been committed to the good earth, those present filed around the grave. Trevor and John, unwilling to create any further incidents, joined the queue and showed due respect. It seemed to Trevor that his friend, Charlie the gravedigger, had done a first-class job; deep hole, clean lines, neat edges.

Perhaps because he was wearing the suit and looked more like a genuine twenty-four carat mourner than anybody present, Trevor's hand was shaken by most of the people there. He knew none of them but nobody considered that strange. He heard himself identified as Cousin Albert's boy, the one who was in the navy, and he was told to his face by a very fat man: 'My word, haven't you grown!'

He was relieved to return to the sanctuary of the yellow van. John sat alongside him.

'Do you know anybody called Hannah?' asked Trevor.

'No.'

'Went well though, didn't it?'

They had agreed on their next step: they would return to Jill's house where the three of them could compare notes of the perplexities of the day.

Over coffee and fig rolls, Jill put the obvious question:

'If it wasn't your funeral, what were you doing there?'

'I'd heard the same story as you,' said John. 'I was supposed to be dead, and I was being buried this afternoon. Seemed too good to miss.'

'Who told you you were dead?' said Trevor.

'Bella, the landlady at the pub. I went in for work last night and she said, what are you doing here? You're dead. Funeral's tomorrow.'

They tried to assemble the information available to them in a neat pattern. John had been away. The day he delivered the tapes to the school he decided, on impulse, to head south where a major jazz festival was taking place. Jill made it quite clear that any talk of the festival was forbidden; they were gathered together strictly to discuss death, rumours of death, and incriminating tapes. That was the agenda and jazz did not qualify, even as Any Other Business.

Several people had heard the news of John's alleged death: Trevor and Jill via the Registrar's office, Bella at the pub, and various of John's friends. In each case the original information had come on the telephone from a man who refused to give a name.

'That would be Peterson,' said Jill.

'Who's Peterson?'

'The man with no name,' said Trevor.

'I see.'

They liked John: he took contradictions in his stride.

'Now tell us about the tape,' said Jill.

'Easy. It was a cock-up. I was supposed to pass it on to a guy called Dave.'

'Dave the wimp?' said Trevor.

'You call him that as well, do you? Poor guy, everybody calls him Dave the wimp. Even before he's been introduced.'

Jill told him how the wimp in question had chased them through the park, in pursuit of the tape, only to be routed by Trevor's show of force. John was puzzled that Trevor should be mentioned in the same sentence as violence, even implicit.

'I've got a black belt,' explained Trevor.

'To hold your trousers up?' asked John.

They really liked John: his sense of humour was warped in all the right directions.

'Now tell us about the tape,' Jill repeated.

'I already did.'

'No. You told us about the cock-up. You didn't tell us what you were doing with it in the first place.'

'Ah.'

John took another fig roll. He needed sustenance before diving into a complicated story.

'Have either of you heard of the PLFWY?'

'Is it a band?' asked Trevor.

'No.'

Trevor turned to Jill.

'Come on, you know all about initials.'

Every week when the *New Statesman* arrived, her conversation was peppered with references, some nice, some nasty, to EEC, WRP, SWAPO, BOSS, PPU, CND, IS and a thousand others. Trevor sometimes retaliated with MCC, BBBC and WASO, but Jill was not excessively interested in cricket, boxing or Belgian jazz.

Jill, though it was one of her specialities, was puzzled by PLFWY.

'I've never heard of it. Sorry.'

'It stands for the Popular Liberation Front of West Yorkshire.'

'No disrespect,' said Jill, 'but you haven't made much of an impact so far. I know most of the political loonies in these parts . . .'

'Many of her best friends . . .' began Trevor.

'Knock it off, smartarse,' said Jill, before resuming her in-depth questioning of John. 'Tell me about its organization. What are your objectives? Have you achieved anything?'

'Sod all.'

'I know the feeling,' said Trevor.

'It was never much of an organization. Do you remember a jazz club called Birdland?'

'In New York?' asked Jill, who sometimes listened to Trevor during his lectures about music, and had absorbed approximately six facts. One of the six was the existence of a famous jazz club called Birdland in New York.

'This one was in Hunslet,' said John, 'round the back of the Flying Ferret. It only lasted a month so suddenly there were seven of us with nothing to do on Thursdays. Dave the wimp said, let's have a political party. That's how the PLFWY was born.'

'Because you had nothing to do on Thursdays?' asked Jill.

'Sounds daft, but in a crazy world, the biggest idiot is bound to be king.'

'Have another fig roll while I work that out,' said Trevor, handing John the packet.

'I've had four already.'

'You've had five but nobody's counting.'

John laughed. 'If you know that joke, Trevor, you must be a music-hall freak.'

'Yes. Jimmy James, Dave Morris, Norman Evans . . . hey, do you know Bobby Thompson? I've got this amazing LP called "The Little Waster" . . .'

Trevor took three paces towards the record shelves before Jill applied his brakes.

'Trevor!'

'Yes?'

'We are not here to swamp our minds with cheerful Geordie humour.'

'It's ethnic. You said so yourself.'

'John is telling us about the Popular Liberation Front of West Yorkshire. When he's done that, we'll have some ethnic humour, if there's time.'

Trevor sat down. John explained the history of the PLFWY.

'Like I said, it began because we had nothing to do on a Thursday. The first week we made some membership cards. The second week we wrote a manifesto. We were non-violent. There were only seven of us, and not a bicep between us, so there was no way we could build a barricade, let alone man it. No chance we could storm the winter palace, because we'd never get over the fence. We decided our target was information.'

'Information?' said Jill. She remembered Sergeant Hobson, the zealous graduate policeman who had unmasked his own commanding officer a year earlier: Hobson's gospel was simple – we live in the age of information. The person with most information would rule the land. It was odd that an ambitious young policeman and a gang of dropouts from a jazz club in Hunslet should reach the same conclusion.

'We didn't want to rule the world,' John continued. 'We didn't want to rule England. But we thought if we aimed at the West Riding of Yorkshire, that would be reasonably within our capabilities. We'd collect all the confidential information we could about what was going on in the West Riding.

Dave the wimp had a brother working for the Council and he used to photocopy minutes of council committee meetings. Mind you, we discovered they were also available on request in the library, so we quit doing that.'

'What about the tape?'

'Well, it seems amazing, but about three times in two years we got it right. We discovered the planners were going to take away some Victorian lampposts in Hall Street, about three months before they did it. We discovered that MP who liked to dress in women's clothes a month before he sold his story to the *Sun*. And we gave a story to a community newspaper about a choirmaster who was a fully paid up member of the National Front.'

'What happened?'

'The newspaper office had its windows kicked in.'

Despite the warmth of her feelings towards John, Jill had to express her doubts.

'No disrespect, but it's all a long way from restoring the land unto the people, so to speak.'

'Right. In fact, we were getting a bit bored with it. Then this tape arrived in the post one day. I played it, heard these guys talking about dumping nuclear waste, realized it was good stuff. Rang Dave, he said he'd pick it up at the pub. Then it got mixed up with your jazz tapes. The rest you know.'

He took the remaining fig roll.

'Where is the tape now?' he asked Jill.

'In a safe place,' said Trevor, beating Jill to the punch. He still had no idea where the tape was.

'Suits me,' said John. 'I didn't enjoy being dead, even if it wasn't true. And Dave didn't enjoy chasing you through the park. It all felt like we were a bit out of our class, you know what I mean? Like sitting in the Ellington band, playing a comb and paper.'

'Everything is now in good hands,' said Jill.

'Good.'

'Does that mean we can have "The Little Waster"?' said Trevor, jumping up and crossing to the record shelves.

'Why aye hinny pet,' said Jill.

The summer term dragged to its close. On sports day, the prayers of staff were answered, resulting in a waterlogged field and cancellation of what Mr Carter called the San Quentin Olympiad.

The summer fayre was marginally more successful in that it took place. It was declared open by the famous ex-student now playing prop forward with Bradford Northern, who turned up late, drunk and incoherent. The event raised £23.76 for the piano fund, mainly because of Yvonne Fairweather's roulette wheel, though it was a technical profit, as the proceeds were stolen from the headmaster's study towards the end of the afternoon.

Generally it was a quiet end of term. Jill and Trevor had no more visits from Peterson, to the best of their knowledge, and there was no news from Sylvia, apart from a postcard bearing a photograph of Lenin and the scribbled note: 'Don't call me, I'll call you. Red Emma lives!'

Twice a week, Mr Wheeler unrolled his map of Holland and gave fierce lectures about famous Dutchmen. The kids moved into a state of permanent confusion about Vermeer and Vermuyden. One of them painted pictures and one built canals – that was all they knew. Jill assisted the chaos with Van Meegeren, who forged pictures, and Trevor added Van der Valk, who once had a television series. Van Morrison was declared null, void and unhelpful to the exercise.

The school trip was to set off on the Monday following the end of term. Mr Wheeler planned the operation like the

Normandy invasion, though with more paperwork. The instructions for D-Day included:

12.00 (Noon) Meet outside main entrance to school.
13.00 (One o'clock) Bus departs PROMPT!!!

Every single item on the information sheet was underlined. Jill argued that this tended to undermine the importance of the vital elements: if everything is underlined then, by definition, nothing is underlined. Questioning the school secretary, she discovered that something was amiss with the reconditioned second-hand electronic typewriter, obtained very cheaply via a parent, and it was impossible to prevent it from underlining, It had a very obstinate microchip and nobody knew how to talk to it.

Jill and Trevor started packing for their holiday at 10.00 (ten o'clock) on the Monday morning. Trevor had finished by 10.10 (ten past ten). Jill looked at what he had done and said it was totally unacceptable.

'The last time I went on a school trip, I took an apple, an orange and a toothbrush.'

'When was that?'

'When I was at school. We went for a long weekend in Paris. To look at some Art.'

'And that's all you took?'

Trevor shrugged.

'Could have used an extra orange.'

She tipped out the odd items he had packed onto the bed and started again. She astonished him with her diagnosis of what would be needed.

'We'll be away seven days and nights. So you'll need seven of everything.'

'Seven toothbrushes?'

'Not toothbrushes. Shirts, socks, underpants.'

'Ah.'

He shuffled. She knew immediately what he was thinking.

'Do I take it you do not have seven pairs of underpants?'

'I doubt it.'

'We'll take what you have and buy some more while we're there.'

'Dutch underpants?'

For some reason the thought bothered him, but he could think of nothing intelligent to say on the subject. He watched in admiration, touching awe, as Jill packed their case. She folded his shirts, with a dexterity and a neatness that passed his understanding by several furlongs.

'Those shirts have never been folded in their lives,' he said.

'Do something useful. Count your socks.'

Trevor counted his socks.

'One pair brown, one pair blueish, one pair black . . . I wore those for the funeral but they'll do another couple of days . . . and a brown one with a thin yellow stripe.'

'One brown sock?'

'It was left over from something.'

They had never been away together and, like supermarket shopping, it revealed more of their differing perceptions of living. For Trevor, the underpants crystallized the challenge. If you lived in daily intimacy with a woman, she was bound to see your underpants. For years they had been his and his alone. There was nothing fundamentally wrong with them. They were simply faded and frayed, as who wouldn't be after all those years? He realized yet another truth of his relationship with Jill: true love, in this case, might mean restocking with underpants, and devoting a little more time and attention to their maintenance.

Jill finished packing and Trevor carried the suitcase down the stairs at 11.07 (seven minutes past eleven), three minutes ahead of their schedule, which allowed twenty minutes for a cup of coffee before leaving for school. It was a half-hour drive to San Quentin High and they had agreed their role throughout the holiday should be to set a good example to the kids, starting by being prompt. They were not utterly devoted to the idea of setting examples, but it struck them as an amusing wheeze that might make the holiday more bearable.

At 11.12 (twelve minutes past eleven) the kettle boiled and at the same moment in time, the cars arrived.

There were three of them, with two men in each. Both the cars and the men were unmarked: no sirens, no flashing blue lights, no screaming of brakes on corners. Five of the men remained silent throughout. The sixth did all the talking.

'Good morning, Mrs Swinburne,' he said at the door. 'You don't mind if we take a look round your house? I advise you not to mind, because in strictly legal terms, you have no choice in the matter.'

'Do you have any form of identification?' asked Jill, in accordance with the many civil rights handbooks she had read, aware as she did so that the other five men were walking past her. Three of them went upstairs. The other two walked into the living room.

The man at the door produced a small card, waved it briefly in the space between them, too briefly for her to read anything that might be written on it. Then he walked past her and into the living room. She followed him.

Trevor was grinding coffee beans in the kitchen. It was another new craft he had learned from Jill. He counted to ten, then switched off the machine. He realized there were three strange men in various parts of the open-plan living and dining areas.

'Er . . .' he said.

Jill walked across to him.

'There are three men in the house,' he said.

'There are three more upstairs. Six altogether.'

'Hell! Do they all want coffee? I'll have to grind some more beans.'

'No. They do not want coffee. Do you?'

The last remark she hurled across the room at the sixth man, the one with the power of speech.

'Coffee will not be necessary, Mrs Swinburne.'

'Who are they?' said Trevor.

'No idea.'

Trevor shrugged and continued to prepare coffee for two. Jill wondered at the complexity of the man. He could easily be thrown off his stride by trivialities like underpants or pineapple chunks, but given a major upheaval like six strange men wandering into the house, he shrugged his shoulders and got on with his own life. He had his own peculiar Geordie version of the English stiff upper lip, a quality he had achieved without high breeding or a public school education; rather with low breeding and a public house education.

They sat on kitchen stools, sipping coffee, and watched the men systematically, carefully and neatly dismantling the house, and reassembling it. Dismantling a house is a long job. At 12.05 (five past twelve) Jill said to the spokesman, 'We should have been at school five minutes ago.'

The man showed no inclination to reply. The telephone rang. Jill crossed the room to answer it. The man put a restraining hand on the receiver. He was not a big man, but gave the impression that no power on earth would be great enough to lift the receiver, not even a thousand Egyptian slaves hardened by double shifts on the Great Pyramid. After a while the ringing stopped.

At 13.05 (five past one) Jill said to the spokesman, 'Our bus left five minutes ago.'

This time the telephone did not ring. It had been dis-mantled, taken apart, degutted and brain-scanned. The men carried a range of small devices, to aid the normal human senses of sight, hearing, smell and touch.

By mid-afternoon, Jill and Trevor were sitting in the living room, while the downstairs men examined the kitchen.

By now the method was becoming clear. In the kitchen, they emptied every container, whether powder or liquid, checked the contents really were as proclaimed by the label, then restored the powder or liquid to its original home. They pulled the washing machine, cooker and dishwasher from their places and carefully examined the spaces behind them. They found a dead mouse, but it was not what they were looking for. They checked every one of Jill's recipe books, from *Albanian Cuisine* to *Zanzibar – An Exciting New Experience*. They seemed to be under the impression that the average book owner is in the habit of hollowing out the pages to conceal incriminating property; such, at any rate, was the basis of their examination.

They also unpacked the case that Jill had so punctiliously packed earlier, examining each item one by one, checking – it seemed to Trevor who was unduly sensitive in these matters – whether the underpants had been hollowed out.

At 15.45 (quarter to four) Trevor said to Jill, 'Do you think they're looking for something?'

'Probably.'

'Thought so.'

Jill was frightened by the men. They were not self-proclaiming bone-breakers. They looked more like civil servants in charcoal grey suits and tasteful ties. Each of them carried a fountain pen in his breast pocket, but a special issue fountain pen giving the impression that if the top were removed, it would release a high velocity laser beam, rather than ink. Their silence was intimidating. Men who carried out orders were bad enough; but men who operated swiftly, without orders, were much worse. They were pre-programmed and resolute, with neatly cut fingernails, all the same length.

Trevor accepted their presence. He knew that everything went away eventually: it was a fact of life. The speaking man was standing nearby, checking the bookshelves. His colleagues had verified earlier that none of the books was hollow; he was now making a note of all the titles and authors.

Trying to relax the atmosphere, Trevor said to the man, 'Do you know a bloke called Peterson? He's in your line of work.'

The man lobbed the question straight back at him, with a tiny change of emphasis: 'Do *you* know Peterson?'

Trevor sensed that for reasons he could not exactly specify, it might be a good idea *not* to know Peterson. A look from Jill seconded his irresolution. It was related to animal fear.

'Only a guy called Oscar. He plays piano. That's who I was thinking of.'

The man obviously did not believe Trevor; he was a professional non-believer. He would want an autopsy on a gift horse.

They left the house at 16.50 (ten to five). They had been in the loft and under floorboards; in every cupboard and every crevice; under the carpets, the underlay and the old newspapers that dwelt beneath the underlay. At no point was there any indication of what they were seeking; nor was there any sign that they had found it, whatever it was. A skilled forensic scientist might have found traces of garlic on their palms, but otherwise there was no visible evidence of their visit, a fact which the man confirmed on departure.

'I should make it quite clear, Mrs Swinburne, that we have not been to your house today. In the unlikely event that you try to challenge this assertion, you will find it impossible to prove. Not one of us has ever visited this area.'

'In that case,' said Jill, 'you'll forgive me if I don't wish you good afternoon.'

She and Trevor watched from the window as the three cars drove away. Jill hoped some of the neighbours might be in the street, so she could have them available as witnesses, in case the unlikely event happened and she wanted to prove the visit had taken place. But the street was deserted. She could not remember any time during the years she had lived in the house when the street had been deserted, especially during a school holiday. It was eerie and alarming.

'Let's go to Holland,' she said.

At 18.35 (twenty-five to seven) a ship sailed along the River Humber, downstream from the Port of Hull, carrying several hundred holiday-makers, truckers and Euro-commercial travellers to the North Sea.

The gallant vessel also bore Mr Wheeler and his school trip. The headmaster stood against the rail, his anger rippling in the breeze, while the kids were dispersed throughout the ferry, exploring with youthful high spirits those areas marked CREW MEMBERS ONLY. They wanted to know why.

Mr Wheeler gazed at the plain of Holderness, lazily stretching out along the North bank, rich agricultural land that held no charms for him. He too wanted to know why, but the question was different: why the hell were Mrs Swinburne and Mr Chaplin not on the boat? He permitted himself an occasional oath in thought, though never in word.

He had telephoned soon after midday but nobody had answered. He had telephoned at one o'clock from school, and at three o'clock and four o'clock from the Port Terminal building. On those occasions a well-spoken male voice had told him: that number is temporarily unavailable.

He was alone with forty young people whose demeanour and discipline would have made each of them a regular member of Genghis Khan's first team squad. By comparison, the *Ancient Mariner* had had it easy.

The ship was a speck on a low horizon, shining brightly as the sun caught it at an angle of thirty glittering degrees. Jill and Trevor watched it sailing out of sight. They were sitting in the van on the dockside. There had never been any chance of their catching it. The van was built for yellowness rather than speed, and it is in any case difficult to check in at 16.00 (four o'clock) when you are sixty miles away at 17.00 (five o'clock). You can only push relativity so far; even Einstein knew that.

'I've missed busses and trains before,' said Trevor, 'but this is the first time I've missed the boat.'

'I should rephrase that,' said Jill.

They braced themselves for a night out in Hull.

Eight

The ferries sailed on a daily basis, and fair stood the wind for Holland as Jill and Trevor went aboard the following evening. Like true Englishpersons, their senses quickened at the prospect of the high seas; strange continents to chart, cheap booze to drink, moonlight dappling the black water plus the tingling fear of a Force Ten gale and comprehensive puking.

Their night out had been a remarkable success, combining good times with in-depth true confessions. Round the back of the bus station they had discovered a theatre made out of an old church, and seen a robust play about Rugby League, written by a weightlifter. They agreed: this could only happen in Hull.

Afterwards they had eaten at a restaurant: not exactly cordon bleu – they were both closed – but a spunky cordon rouge curry house. Between forkfuls of his beloved vindaloo, Trevor, for once, provoked the in-depth conversation.

'Why did you let them?' he asked.

'Difficult question, since I don't know what you're talking about.'

'Those men. They walked in. They took the house apart from top to bottom. And you didn't do anything. What about all those books you've got. What to do if you get busted, volumes one to fifty-three?'

'Hand on heart, Trevor, I was shit-scared.'

He stared at her. They had talked more things through

than he'd had school dinners, but at no time had she ever confessed to fear.

'Scared of them? They were blokes in suits. They looked like an annual outing from a firm of solicitors.'

'When they first arrived, I watched as they walked in. Two of them had left their jackets unfastened. They had guns, Trevor. Little revolvers.'

'Ah.'

He pushed his plate to one side, defeated by sheer volume of rice.

'But . . . they wouldn't have used them, would they? I mean, people like them don't go around shooting people like us. Do they?'

He considered his own question, failed to find a satisfactory answer, so asked it again, to fill the silence.

'Do they?'

'You should read some history books. Millions of people have died with those words on their lips: they don't shoot people like us, do they?'

'Oh come on,' Trevor said, a little impatiently by his standards, and therefore beatifically by anybody else's. 'Nobody's going to shoot you because of a tape. Where is the tape, anyway?'

'In a safe place.'

'Fancy some pudding?'

She ignored his invitation.

'Peterson was just a big loudmouth by comparison. Those men were real professionals. I believe they left their jackets unfastened knowing I would see they were carrying guns. They wanted me to be shit-scared and I was.'

'OK. We'll skip the pudding. We'll have a cuddle at the hotel.'

They had found a jolly hotel, made out of an old warehouse, where the management was prepared to accept Trevor's credit card as a substitute for legal tender. There was a disco down below that vibrated well into the night, and, though there was no duvet, Jill and Trevor did the same. They cuddled against the thought of being shit-scared, and out of their fear came forth sweetness.

Cabin number C114 was as exclusive as it sounded. It had two bunks, one above the other, and a washbasin. This left enough room for a bar of soap and two small towels. They agreed the cabin was small because the designers needed to leave space for the ship's engine room, which seemed to be next door but on both sides, as well as above and below.

They decided to eat, drink and be merry, for tomorrow they might find Mr Wheeler and the school trip.

'We'll probably find him floating face downwards in a canal, if I know Yvonne Fairweather,' said Trevor.

'Easy with the death jokes. You know I'm sensitive.'

She was smiling as she said it. She was getting better.

In the dining room was a self-service buffet as long as a Tolstoy novel. Jill pointed out the best fibres, and Trevor took no notice, his mind on other, more pressing matters. When they sat down, Jill realized what he had done.

'Trevor! You've made a face!'

Not only that, he was proud of it. A sausage for the nose, tomatoes for the eyes, a rosebud mouth made from a prettily sliced radish, green lettuce hair, a formidable beard of potato salad and anchovy eyebrows.

'Who does it look like? Go on . . . who does it look like?'

He turned his plate around so she could see better.

'Father Christmas?'

'Slim Gaillard.'

'Who?'

She should have known better after all this time.

'Jazz musician and famous eccentric singer. Composer of such songs as "Flat Foot Floogie", "Matzoh Balls", "Cement Mixer" and "The Avocado Seed Soup Symphony Parts One and Two". Also there's a chapter about him in "On The Road" by Jack Kerouac.'

'Trevor.'

'Yes?'

'Eat your dinner.'

The wine waiter arrived at their table. He was pushing a small trolley and had a Liverpool accent.

'Red or white?'

Trevor Chaplin no longer trembled at the sight of a wine waiter; he approached them with almost the same degree of assurance that he set about a dovetail joint.

'I think a bottle of Frascati would work well in conjunction with Slim Gaillard's beard, don't you?'

'Red or white?'

'White please.'

They clinked their glasses of *vin blanc ordinaire*. The glasses too were pretty *ordinaire*, toughened against the possibility of gales and large outings of master builders.

'Think of a toast,' said Jill.

'Us?'

'You can do better than that.'

'Dutch duvets?'

'Safe places.'

They agreed on that: safe places. Before the wine had passed Trevor's lips, he stared into the middle distance, like a Chekovian heroine dreaming of Moscow.

'What's wrong?' said Jill.

'I know that face.'

'It's Slim Wotsit.'

'Not that face. I've eaten that face. I mean *that* face.'

He pointed out a man sitting across the other side of the

room, toying apathetically with a bowl of soup. He was clinging precariously to his late fifties. Wrinkles criss-crossed his face like a major intersection on a narrow-gauge railway. His eyes shone like tiny pools of ketchup.

'Who is he?' asked Jill, averting her gaze, with some relief.

'Can't remember.'

'In which case you don't know him.'

'I know the face. Just can't remember his name. I wonder if he was a footballer?'

'Heaven forbid.'

It was too late. Trevor lurched into a prolonged reminiscence of soccer heroes from his childhood, trying to work out which of those healthy, fresh-faced, red-kneed young athletes had turned into the wrinkled man opposite.

'Does it matter?' said Jill. 'He looks like a prune. He probably is a prune.'

'I know his face. Wonder if he's one of the Milburns or one of the Charltons?'

Jill put a stop to the anthology of old cigarette cards by suggesting they go to the bar.

The bar was like a hunk of Las Vegas, bought cheap but not all that cheap. It had a large bow window overlooking the blunt end of the ship. Between that and the serious drinking section was a dance floor, large enough to accommodate edited highlights of a formation dancing team, with music supplied by a very tired man playing an organ. After the first two drinks, Trevor realized the man was playing the same half-dozen Beatles' hits in endless rotation. He pointed this out to Jill, who was less inclined to blame the man for his musical limitations than to assume that there was some underlying psychological problem.

'It's not his fault if he only knows six tunes. He probably had an unhappy childhood.'

'I bet he knows "Viva España" as well. We'll have that

before they call time. But if he plays "My Way" I'm going for a walk around the deck. I'll check the lifeboats. Maybe we should check them anyway.'

'Have another drink.'

The drinks were noticeably cheaper than on shore and most of the passengers, in consequence, were proportionately pisseder. Jill and Trevor saw no compelling reason for taking a stand on temperance at this point in their lives.

Trevor returned to the table with another vodka-and-tonic and another pint of bitter.

'Your wrinkled man's about to do something,' Jill said.

Trevor looked across at the nominal bandstand. It was at the same level as the surrounding floor and showed no signs of revolving. He had to stand up to see what was happening. The wrinkled man was opening a black instrument case. He brought out a saxophone, while having a murmured conversation with the organ player.

'Whyebuggerman! I know who that is!' said Trevor, sitting down.

'One of the Milburns or one of the Charltons?'

'He's a tenor player. Used to play with the Heath band. I saw him at the City Hall in Newcastle. He played with all of them. Vic Lewis, Jack Parnell, Dankworth, the Kirchins. . .'

'Do I take it that ageing prune is some sort of musician?'

'Yes. He plays tenor sax. He's great. Oh, what's his name? He's got this lovely sound, all furry. He breathes all the time.'

'I breathe all the time. What's so special about that?'

'Like Ben Webster. You can hear him breathing.'

She moved her chair around the table so that she was sitting closer to him, ostensibly so that she too could see the musical event that was still being planned. She placed an affectionate arm on Trevor's shoulders.

'Last night I could hear you breathing, Trevor.'

'Give over, man.'

It bothered her when Trevor called her 'man' in the Geordie style, though it could get even more complicated. His record was, 'Hadaway man, woman, hinny, pet.'

The organ player and the wrinkled man had some trouble in finding any kind of common repertoire. It seemed the tenor sax player's ideological scruples ruled out all of the six Beatles' tunes. Eventually, on a count of four, they stumbled into a bossa nova. Trevor's expert analysis was that the wrinkled man was playing 'The Girl from Ipanema' while the organist was playing a samba with a passing similarity to 'The British Grenadiers'.

They finished their two tunes at approximately the same time. Trevor applauded enthusiastically. Jill joined in, out of sympathy. Nobody else on the entire ship took any notice at all.

'Philistines!' Trevor growled.

'No, I think most of them are English,' said Jill, throwing one of his old jokes back in his face.

'Sam Bentley, that's his name. Sam Bentley. Hey, that was great, wasn't it?'

'I'm sorry, Trevor, but I didn't actually think it was very good.'

'That's the organ player's fault. He's never passed his test. Doesn't know which is the brake and which is the clutch. Shhh!'

He put his fingers to his lips as the two men started another tune. It purported to be a blues. Sam Bentley's tone was as breathy as Trevor had promised, but the organ player went into overdrive, and the result was a million light years away from the Mississippi Delta; closer to Saturday night in the Old Kent Road. When they finished, Trevor clapped alone, out of loyalty to a distant echo from his lost adolescence.

Sam Bentley put his saxophone in the case and left the

bandstand, with a perfunctory scowl at the organ player. He found an empty stool at the end of the bar, put the instrument case at his feet and ordered a quadruple Scotch.

'Shall we invite him over for a drink?' said Trevor.

'I think he's already got a drink.'

'Seems a shame, a fellow like that. Drinking on his own. The man's a legend.'

'It's often the fate of legends to drink alone. Ho Chi-Minh, Aristotle, Neville Chamberlain, Louis Pasteur, Ethelred the Unready, all famous solitary drinkers, and legends to boot.'

Jill enjoyed beating him over the head with lists of names: it was sweet and loving revenge for the footballers and jazz musicians she had suffered.

'All right,' said Trevor, 'let's invite him over for a drink *not* because he's a legend, but because . . . with that amount of wrinkles he must have had an unhappy childhood.'

'You swine!'

'Game, set and match to Trevor?'

The vodka had taken effect. She acknowledged he had beaten her at her own game.

'Why don't you ask him over for a drink?' Jill said. 'Maybe we can talk a few things through.'

'Great idea.'

Trevor wandered over to the bar and tapped the great man on the shoulder, very carefully. His equilibrium looked in bad shape as he swayed on the stool, like a delicately balanced wooden parrot.

'Excuse me, Mr Bentley, would you like to join us in a drink?'

'Bastard,' said Bentley.

Even to a devoted fan like Trevor, it seemed on the ungracious side.

'Howay man, all I said was, would you like to join us in a drink?'

143

Bentley swivelled on his stool, and with an almost audible effort looked at Trevor, who was sure he heard the eyes creak with the unaccustomed effort of focusing.

'You're not the bastard. *He's* the bastard.'

He flicked his head a couple of millimetres in the direction of the dance floor, the sudden movement almost dislodging him from the stool. He was no sort of athlete. Trevor steadied him. He resumed the static position and static was what he needed to be.

Trevor tried out his theory about the identity of the bastard.

'The organ player? Is he the bastard?'

'You heard him play?'

'Yes. I heard him play.'

'Message ends. Bastard. I'll have a Scotch.'

The invitation had penetrated at last, and obviously made good sense.

'Scotch please,' Trevor called to the barman, who was being swamped by a bulk order for port-and-lemon from a WI outing. Somewhere in the bar women were singing 'By The Light Of The Silvery Moon', in a commendable and successful effort to drown the organist's version of Norwegian Wood: not so much playing it as felling it.

Trevor realized Jill was looking at him from the table with a look that said, are you bringing that prune with you or not? He tried to respond with a look that said, I'm waiting to be served, and besides the prune is smashed out of his skull and if I walk away he'll fall over.

'A Scotch please,' he called again, trying to be firm and masterly.

'A large one,' added Bentley, still alert to the fundamentals of his existence.

'I heard you play with the Heath band,' said Trevor,

hoping to guide the conversation in the direction of his passion.

'Man, that was a great band. Have one with me.'

The barman slid the Scotch towards Bentley.

'Make that two!'

It became clear that the great man, with years of practice behind him, was supremely skilled at giving the illusion of buying drinks for everybody in the house, without at any time putting his hand in his pocket.

Trevor paid for the drinks, then realized, too late, that he had forgotten to buy a drink for Jill. The barman was once more swamped, this time a block booking of several gallons of Australian lager for a rugby club. Somewhere in the bar men were singing how they all put it in together, while elsewhere the WI chorus had developed into 'Mother Kelly's Doorstep'. The two songs, in conjunction with the organist's approximate version of 'Penny Lane', sounded like a new oratorio by Stockhausen.

'And didn't I hear you play with the Tubby Hayes band?'

'Man, that was a great band,' said Bentley.

He did not seem sure whether he had played with the Tubby Hayes band, and Trevor, on reflection, had doubts too. He also had growing doubts about the merits of close encounters with the legendary.

Jill tapped him on the shoulder.

'Having fun?'

'Quiet. You'll wake him up.'

Bentley had declined into a gentle stupor, his head resting on Trevor's shoulder. The arm reached out periodically, picked up the glass, and fed Scotch into the mouth: the boozing mechanisms worked with great efficiency, quite independently of the other functions of the body. It was awe-inspiring in its way.

'I thought I'd take a stroll around the deck. Check the lifeboats. Are you coming?'

'I can't,' said Trevor, 'he'll fall off the stool.'

'It's your choice. I'll do a couple of laps and see you back here.'

'Mind how you go,' said Trevor, stretched between conflicting loyalties.

'Don't worry. If a strange man offers me chocolates, I'll hold out for the coffee cream.'

It was a balmy night on deck and barmy too. The air was warm and fragrant, as promised in the travel brochure, and like tropical flowers with only twenty-four hours to live, shipboard romances blossomed in every nook and cranny.

On her second circuit of the deck, Jill did a body-swerve straight from the George Best handbook to avoid a middle-aged couple grappling with their respective mid-life crises, and collided with Peterson, who was leaning on No 3 lifeboat.

'Good heavens,' she said. 'Mr Peterson, the man with no name.'

She was almost pleased to see him. At least he was not six men in grey suits and shoulder holsters.

'Mrs Swinburne. It's lovely to see you again.'

Lovely was an odd word to use, she thought.

'Am I under surveillance or is this just a silly coincidence of the kind that makes life interesting as we pass through the vale of tears?'

She paused for breath. Three vodkas generally made her verbose; four vodkas and the words came out in like quantity, but in the wrong order.

'Yes and no,' said Peterson. The answer made little sense to her but so, in retrospect, did her question.

'I see.'

He stared out into the blackness of the North Sea, trying, it seemed to Jill, to look soulful, almost willing the breeze to ruffle his hair in an appealing fashion. The hair was thick, brown and neatly cut. It had been layered, unlike Trevor's, which always looked heaped.

'Mrs Swinburne. I need to talk to you.' There was an urgency in his voice.

'Go ahead,' she said. 'I'm not bugged, even if you are.'

'Please don't be flippant.'

'I'm on my holidays, I've had three vodkas and if I want to be flippant, no power on earth will stop me.'

He added a sigh, supplementary to the soulful gazing and hair-ruffling. 'Mrs Swinburne.'

'Mr Peterson?'

She felt it was a good idea to fill the soulful silences with sound, if only a meaningless repetition of his name.

'I love you, Mrs Swinburne.'

'Huh?'

'I love you.'

'Don't give me that sort of talk. I want to see the colour of your coffee creams.'

Trevor had fed Bentley with two more glasses of Scotch and the wrinkled man had insisted on his companion joining him. He was still leaning on Trevor, but the support was now more mutual. They resembled a pair of bookends in an illiterate household.

'I think . . . once . . . I saw you playing . . . City Hall, Newcastle . . . with the . . . Dankworth band,' said Trevor, taking a run at the word Dankworth, which was a bit heavy on syllables at this stage in his evening.

'Man, that was a great band.'

'A great band,' echoed Trevor, finding echoes easier than originality.

'Didn't you see me playing in it? City Hall? Somewhere?'

'Right.'

'Yes, all right, if you insist, I will have another.'

Trevor was beginning to like the legendary Sam Bentley. He was beginning to like everybody, distillers in particular.

Peterson sat on a forgotten deckchair. Jill leant on the ship's rail, keeping distance between them. The man with no name talked it through.

'The people I work for give the orders. The orders were to maintain surveillance on you and recover a tape recording of information vital to the nation's security. I carried out my orders. I have failed, so far, to recover the tape. But coming into close contact with you, I realized there is more to life than maintaining surveillance. All the humanity, all the tenderness, all the love that I'd buried, under orders . . . all that came bursting out. We are trained not to have feelings. Not to have emotions. You taught me there is another way, Mrs Swinburne.'

It sounded to Jill like dialogue from a lousy movie. She was tempted to respond in kind: seems to me, Mr Peterson, you've been running away all your life but what you've been running away from is . . . (pause) . . . yourself.

What she actually said was, 'Cor.'

'That's a rather inadequate response. I open my heart to you and all you can say is "Cor".'

Jill was playing for time. She could see a possibility shining clearly through vodka fumes. Though she had no feelings of tenderness towards Peterson, she might be able to play on his feelings to translate the nonsense of surveillance and searches into plain English like ordinary people use. She played a card marked Trevor.

'You must realize, Mr Peterson, that I'm already living with somebody.'

'Mr Chaplin.'

'Yes, he answers to Mr Chaplin.'

'He's not worthy of you, Mrs Swinburne.'

She thought about this for a moment. Peterson pushed harder on the same pedal.

'You know he isn't.'

Jill shook her head. 'I don't agree. He's a very kind man.'

'He's scruffy. He doesn't even walk properly. He slouches. He's round-shouldered. And he needs a haircut.'

'Yes, I agree with all of that.'

'So?'

'So . . . nothing.'

Peterson repeated the sighing routine, took out a packet of cigarettes, offered her one.

'I don't.'

He took out a cigarette for himself.

'And under no circumstances could I have anything to do with a man who smoked cigarettes,' said Jill, thinking: you really do play a mean game, Swinburne.

'I don't smoke cigarettes,' said Peterson. 'I throw them over the sides of ships, one at a time, at hourly intervals.'

He threw the cigarette over the side. He may have been a tall, muscular, trained killer, but he was a quick thinker too, when motivated by love. He put the packet away.

'Mr Peterson – ' Jill began.

'I'd rather you called me Neville.'

Jill winced. She found it difficult to call anybody Neville. There had been a boy of that name in her class when she started school, a charmless urchin who ate worms and looked at girls' knickers. He had once looked at hers, while eating a worm, and every Neville who had floated into her orbit in the years following had paid a terrible price.

On the other hand, the security of the nation was at stake, one way or the other, and sacrifices had to be made.

'Neville,' she said, quickly and quietly, 'there are things I have to tell you. Yesterday, our house was invaded by six men in grey suits. They said they were looking for a tape. They failed to find it. But they stayed for six hours and searched the place from top to bottom. They were carrying guns. Are they anything to do with you?'

'Doesn't sound like our lot. We don't work in sixes.'

'Thank you. Have you just broken the Official Secrets Act, telling me that?'

'Probably. I'm past caring, Mrs Swinburne.'

He looked at her sharply, waiting for the invitation to call her Jill. None came. She was in her investigative mood and she sensed she had the wind behind her.

'When you say . . . not your lot, does that mean there's another lot?'

'Well . . . obviously.'

'But you say your lot are protecting the nation's security.'

'Yes.'

'This other lot, the lot who work in sixes . . . are they protecting the nation's security as well?'

'Yes.'

'The same nation? I mean, they're not American or South African or some mysterious foreign power? They are, if you'll pardon the expression, British?'

'Yes.'

She felt the need to summarize. The confirmations were flying by too quickly. She had to hold on to something.

'Hang on,' she said, 'you're telling me the British nation has so much security to protect that it needs several lots of people like you to protect it?'

'Yes. There are quite a lot of . . . lots.'

'A lot of lots.'

'Yes.'

'Sort of MI5 to MI35 inclusive?'

'That's the principle of the thing. Safety in numbers. Checks and counter-checks.'

He was happy to be talking to her at all, but uneasy about the direction of the conversation. Most of his vows of official secrecy were shattered, a little pile of dust, where once had stood a mighty tower of integrity and loyalty to the code of silent watchers.

'May we change the subject, Mrs Swinburne?'

'Why? It's very interesting.'

'I've already said far too much.'

It was another lousy line from another lousy movie. Jill wanted to say: one day we will be free, your nation and mine, but feared he wouldn't have a clue what she was talking about. He saved her the trouble of finding an adequate response by frowning, adjusting his profile, taking out the cigarettes and, as he caught the look on her face, throwing another one over the side.

'Mrs Swinburne . . .'

'It's only twenty minutes since you threw the last one over the side. You should try to cut down.'

'Please, Mrs Swinburne, may I be permitted to hope?'

'Hope?'

She had spent too long at San Quentin High. The concept of hope was long forgotten.

'May I hope that one day you might look on me with, if not love, at least a morsel of affection?'

'I can find affection for most people, except those who want to blow up the planet. And their paid lackeys.'

Peterson knew when people were talking about him.

'You mean me, don't you?'

'Of course I mean you, you soft pillock.'

It was intended to hurt and it did. Jill was willing to wound and not afraid to strike. Peterson got up from the deckchair and crossed to the ship's rail, maintaining a respectful distance between his loved one and himself.

'A lackey? Is that how I seem to you?'

'Yes.'

He obviously wanted her to think he was going to climb over the rail and consign his personal crisis to Providence and the North Sea.

Jill, having extracted as much information as she could cope with on such a night as this, was growing bored.

'Mr Peterson,' she said.

'A few minutes ago you called me Neville.'

'Mr Neville Peterson, a long time ago I left my scruffy, round-shouldered cohab in the bar with a wrinkled saxophone player. I really should go back. Trevor will be worrying about me.'

'If he's worrying about you, why hasn't he come looking?'

'That's another reason.'

The bar was like a cup-tie between Sodom and Gomorrah, to decide who should play Armageddon in the final. The organist was playing a selection of Beatles' hits. He was the only element to have remained constant all night. The WI party was singing about the Wild West Show while the rugby players' voices rattled the bulwarks with 'Jerusalem'.

Jill and Peterson walked in from the boat deck, as the organist started to play 'Michelle'.

'May I have this dance?' he said.

'Why do you want to dance?'

It seemed an absurd and irrelevant notion: for a start, they would have to decide which of the various tunes they should dance to.

'It would be a memory to take away. I suspect we'll never meet again.'

He was so mawkish, she gave way, calculating that two laps of the dance floor would provide a good sight of the room thereby allowing her to find Trevor.

'All right. On condition we never meet again.'

She thought, that would be a decent line for a lousy movie.

Trevor and the wrinkled jazz legend had propelled themselves from the bar to a corner table, taking a bottle with them. They had a joint theory about cutting out the middleman. Neither of them understood what it meant but they had moved beyond understanding into another galaxy of communication.

'Saw you once,' said Trevor, 'playing with . . . John Philip Sousa's marching band . . . they were . . . marching and playing . . . a march, as I recall. "The Tarzan stripes for ever".'

'Man, that was a great band.'

From somewhere about his person, Bentley had found a pair of dark glasses. He was in his 1940s New York bebop mode. It was truly a night for adolescent fantasy revisited.

'Also saw you playing with . . . Johann Sebastian . . . Brahms . . . and his Band of Renown.'

Bentley was preparing his mouth to confirm the greatness of the band when Trevor looked up to see Jill dancing with Peterson, the man with no name. The music, insofar as it had any perceptible quality, was smoochy and Peterson was smooching. Jill was not smooching, but her partner was a big strong man and, in strict terms, she was being smooched.

'Man, that was a really cool band, that Brahms,' said Bentley as Trevor got up. His support removed, the heavy-breathing legend of the tenor sax slid gently to the ground.

153

Trevor stumbled two yards to the dance floor, tapped Peterson on the shoulder, and said, without any idea where the words came from, 'Unhand that woman, sir!'

'Huh?' said Peterson.

'Trevor!'

Too late Jill tried to stop him. Trevor swung a mighty blow. It was the first time in his life that he had hit anybody. Perhaps for that reason the punch was a perfect one, refined in the juices of a thousand small frustrations and resentments. It struck Peterson on the point of the jaw and he fell to the floor.

'Trevor!'

Jill did not know whether to laugh, cry, call for an ambulance or start a peace petition.

Trevor took a unilateral decision. He too collapsed in a heap, overcome by emotion and the sweet wine of bonny Scotland. Jill looked around her at Bentley, Peterson and Trevor. Suddenly she was in a second feature Western, with only her and the organist left alive.

Nine

'You don't remember hitting anyone?'

Trevor shook his head and instantly realized his mistake. His head and his entire internal system felt as if they had been pumped full of cavity-wall insulation.

'Do you remember getting drunk with that wrinkled prune?'

'It hurts when I move my head and it hurts when I talk,' Trevor said, his voice a husk of its usual self.

They were on a coach, taking them from the Dutch Europort to the heart of downtown Rotterdam where they planned to find Mr Wheeler and the San Quentin High School trip. How soon and how hard they tried was subject to discussion and an improvement in Trevor's physical state.

'All right,' said Jill, 'we'll make it easy. Hold up one finger for yes, two fingers for no. Does it hurt to move your fingers?'

He held up three fingers, by way of a research project. His stomach heaved, but the two items were unrelated.

'You held up three fingers, Trevor. Does that mean yes, no or undecided?'

Trying to decide how many fingers he should raise in answer to the question was the worst mental agony Trevor had been through since trying to remember the key dates of the American War of Independence in O-level history. He had failed that too. Unable to pick his way through the swamp of Jill's logic, he held up one finger, because that was easiest.

'Good,' she said.

Trevor relaxed: he had got the first one right.

'Now, Trevor, tell me . . . do you remember going to the bar to have a drink with a saxophone player who, you said, was a heavy-breathing living legend?'

He raised one finger, slowly.

'Would I be right in thinking that while I was away, checking the lifeboats, you got smashed out of your skull?'

Again he raised one finger, though he scowled at her cruelty in reminding him of his skull at a time when it was giving him such trouble.

'Do you remember me getting fed up because you'd abandoned me at the table, and telling you I was going for a stroll around the deck?'

He raised one finger. He half-remembered odd incidents but also realized a more important truth: as long as he held up one finger, whatever Jill said, she would carry on talking quietly and not probe too deeply. It was the line of least resistance and he was in no mood for resistance.

'Do you remember towards the end of the evening, when I came back into the bar? Do you remember me dancing with somebody? Do you remember who it was?'

One finger.

'You remember it was Peterson? The man with no name?'

One finger.

'Good. So you do remember what happened last night?'

His finger was tired and he escaped briefly into the spoken word.

'What happened last night?' he said.

Jill's immediate strategy was practical and straightforward. They would check in at the hotel where the San Quentin party was staying, and she would fill Trevor with black coffee and put him to bed for the day. According to Mr Wheeler's itinerary the mob would have left town for a day trip to the Hague at 10.00 (ten o'clock) and it was now almost eleven.

It was not one of the great hotels of Europe. It had one and a half stars and was RAC recommended with an asterisk and three pages of footnotes. Though not in a red-light district in the truly professional sense, the street seemed littered with enthusiastic amateurs working the early shift.

The hotel manager was called Pronk. He was a large, bucolic, stage Dutchman, with a red face. He would have looked good on a cheese wrapping, against a background of windmills. Across the desk of the small lobby, he was less appealing.

'You should have a room for us. We are with the school party that arrived yesterday.'

'Vith Mister Veeler?'

Hell's teeth, thought Trevor, who was leaning against a broken coffee machine where Jill had propped him, we come all this way and the place is thick with funny foreigners.

'Yes,' said Jill, 'we are with Mr Wheeler's party.'

'They have departed to The Hague.'

'I know that, Mr . . . .'

'Pronk. My name is Pronk. Manager and overseer.'

Funny foreigners with funny names, thought Trevor; I wonder if Mr Pronk thinks Chaplin is a funny name?

'Well, Mr Pronk, I know that Mr Wheeler has taken the children on a trip to The Hague, but they will be back this evening and you should have a room booked for us, and we would like to use it immediately so that we can wash ourselves and rest our bodies.'

Like all conscientious English people abroad, Jill felt the

157

need to explain everything in vast and irrelevant detail, so that all speeches sounded like phrases from a guidebook, badly glued together.

'They have gone to The Hague, but they vill not return.'

'I'm sorry?'

'I have told them. They vill not return. Take your baggages and go.'

The truth dawned on Jill with the inevitability of classical tragedy. Trevor was less sensitive to what was going on. After a period of calm, a tidal wave was sweeping through his intestines.

'May I be quite clear about this, Mr Pronk? Mr Wheeler and his school party have left the hotel? They are not coming back?'

'I have told them. They must never return.'

'Do you know where they are staying tonight?'

'I have told them. That is Mr Veeler's problem.'

Jill had a very good idea what the answer to her next question would be, in essence if not in detail, but asked anyway.

'What exactly happened, Mr Pronk?'

'The children are animals. They release my fire extinguishers upon old men and women. They write sexual and erotic slogans upon many of my walls. They make noises and frighten people in the street. They frighten my Doberman, who protects me against evil-doers, and he vill not leave his kennel, even now. They climb upon my several roofs. They steal cigarettes from the machine, also breeding control devices from my lavatories.'

'That all makes sense,' said Jill.

'Lavatories,' said Trevor. 'Ask him about the lavatories.'

The voice was louder than when he was on the bus, but the texture was that of a blunt saw grinding teak.

'Is your husband ill?' asked Mr Pronk.

'He would like to use your lavatory.'

'The lavatories vere wandalized.'

For a moment, Jill and Trevor thought Verwanderlized was the name of the local plumber, then translation permeated.

'Vandalized or not, I think he would welcome any kind of receptacle,' said Jill. She had neither the heart nor the time to explain that Trevor was not really her husband. Pronk might find it difficult to cope with cohabitation, both the word and the morality.

'Lavatories are there,' said Pronk, indicating a door at the end of a narrow, green corridor. Trevor covered the distance between the coffee machine and the lavatory door with a velocity that would have impressed Jesse Owens.

While Trevor was away, Jill tried to elicit from Pronk where he thought the San Quentin party might transfer their attentions for the remainder of their stay. He gave her a tourist guide with a list of star-and-a-half hotels.

'But I think they vill not be velcome once the police have reported.'

'Police?'

'Last night ve call the police. Now the police vill issue varnings to innkeepers throughout the city.'

Jill pondered the implications of police varnings: if the San Quentin party found itself homeless and on the streets, in a city with a population of over six hundred thousand, she and Trevor could hardly be blamed if they failed to find them. If finding them was going to be near-impossible anyway, it would make a great deal of sense not to bother trying. She and Trevor, once he was recovered from his *mal de prune*, might as well just have a good time, and take the consequences at the start of the autumn term.

'Thank you very much, Mr Pronk,' she said, smiling.

'You're velcome.'

Jill and Trevor went on a round trip of the canals. It had been recommended by Mr Pronk, whose attitude towards them had softened once he discovered they were leaving. He told them a canal trip was an excellent way of learning the geography of his fine city, slowly and painlessly; and it was a highly regarded form of hangover cure with the neighbourhood boozers.

The news had obviously spread, and there were long queues of tourists from all nations, but after an hour Jill and Trevor found themselves setting out on their voyage of relaxation, tranquillity and optional scholarship. The guide, a young student of indeterminate sex, explained points of historical interest in English, German and Italian, all of them impeccable. Here once lived a great painter, there once lived a great scientist, here once lived a great musician, there once lived a great surgeon. They would pass under seventy-three bridges, including those they would pass under twice, because of the circular logic of the tour. S/he would be delighted to answer any questions.

The water was marbled smooth and Trevor, sitting at the side of the boat, murmured to Jill.

'I've got a question.'

'What is it?'

'Ask him or her whether anybody's ever been seasick on a canal cruise.'

'You're not to be sick, Trevor. You can't possibly have anything left to puke with.'

'Is it all right if I go to sleep?'

'Go to sleep.'

Trevor dozed off, leaning on Jill's shoulder. A benign, silver-haired American sitting nearby smiled at them. He had the comforting look of a man who had modelled himself on Spencer Tracy.

'That's a sweet picture. Are you on your honeymoon?'

'In a manner of speaking.'

It was too complicated to explain, even to a man like Spencer Tracy.

The guide explained that here lived a painter famous for his interiors and there lived another painter also famous for his interiors, and soon they would pass under the twelfth of the seventy-three bridges.

It occurred to Jill, with the arrogance of the tourist, that behind every Dutch exterior lay a Dutch interior waiting for some bugger to paint it; whereas at home you could wait months for a painter to show up. She was tired and the mind was beginning to slip.

As they passed under the twelfth bridge a cheerful voice called 'Smile please!' in three consecutive languages and the passangers, Trevor excepted, smiled in an upwards direction. A young man leaning over the parapet took a photograph, then jumped on a bicycle and sped away in a cloud of urgency. The guide explained that copies of the photographs would be available, modestly priced, at the end of the cruise, as a memorial to their voyage. It was the first time his/her command of English had deviated from perfection.

It was as the boat sailed under the thirteenth bridge that Jill saw the two men. They were leaning over the parapet, they wore grey suits and they were looking at her. She blinked and subjected her feelings to immediate, cold, Swinburnian analysis. The night before she had slept for only two hours. Trevor had been up and down, noisily and frequently, at twenty-minute intervals. Therefore she was tired. Therefore she had imagined the two men on the bridge. They were simply two men on a bridge, who happened to be wearing grey suits, and who happened to look as if they were looking at her. It was obvious when she thought about it.

There were two more men on the fifteenth bridge, also in

grey suits, also looking at her; and there were two more on the seventeenth. They seemed to favour odd numbers.

There was a gap before the nineteenth bridge, while the boat chugged into the harbour so that the guide could explain the maritime heritage of the Dutch and how this was continued even to this day. Here was a large ocean-going oil tanker and there was a large ocean-going oil tanker, each capable of carrying ten megamillion megalitres of crude mega-oil.

They sailed back into the heart of the city, under the eighteenth bridge, where the population was an average socio/econo mix of humanity. On the nineteenth bridge stood the original two men in grey suits, looking down at Jill.

She did rapid calculations: if the original two men had first appeared at the thirteenth bridge and had now reappeared at the nineteenth, did that mean six men altogether, working in relays?

The guide droned on with practised precision: here lived a great painter, famous for his Dutch interiors, there lived a great explorer, famous for his African interiors, here comes a great bridge . . . .

And if it's an odd number, thought Jill, there will be two men on it, in grey suits, with concealed revolvers, looking at me, and Trevor's asleep and I do not know what to do.

When the boat passed under the thirty-seventh bridge, she was certain that her arithmetic was correct. There were six men, working in pairs. They looked alarmingly like the six men who had visited the house only two days earlier. There was another possibility, equally disturbing: she might be going round the bend. Perhaps the vodka was rotting her sensory perception.

It was not much of a choice. On the one hand, being pursued across Europe by six anonymous armed men; on the other hand, sliding into madness with alcoholic poisoning as a fringe benefit. It was inevitable, in the circumstances, that her face carried the odd trace of anxiety. The silver-haired American noticed.

'You look a little worried, ma'am.'

'Well . . .'

She shrugged, reluctant to share irrational fears with a total stranger who might, for all she knew, be a paid-up member of the Ku Klux Klan; but he did look very much like Spencer Tracy in his priestly mode, and she had only slept for two hours the night before and the voice was warm and reassuring.

'I've lived a long time on this good earth,' said Mr Tracy, 'and I know when I look into somebody's eyes and there are things troubling those eyes and the sweet soul that dwells within.'

'Really?'

'Oh yes. I see in your eyes a nightmare so close you can almost touch it.'

Jill wondered whether the man was recuperating from a Scott Fitzgerald transplant.

'I would be honoured to share your anxiety. As we say where I live, an anxiety shared is a psychiatrist's bill saved.'

Trevor showed no sign of waking up before the start of the football season. Jill, though reluctant to cast herself as the weak woman seeking protection with the silver-haired father-figure, owned up.

'There are some men watching me.'

'Pardon the chauvinism, ma'am, but that is totally understandable.'

'It isn't quite like that. Primeval lust I can cope with. This is different. This is quiet men in grey suits standing on every alternate bridge, looking at me. Armed men.'

Spencer Tracy let out a low whistle. 'You're sure about this?'

163

'Watch. This next bridge is the forty-third. I promise you, there will be two men in grey suits looking down.'

The guide informed the passengers that the next bridge was designed by a great engineer, whose contribution to bridge-building techniques was acknowledged by bridge builders in all four corners of the world. S/he did not mention the two men in grey suits who stood on the bridge, looking down at Jill.

Spencer Tracy saw the men.

'Sweet Jesus,' he said, 'and pardon me if you're a devout and deeply Christian person.'

'I'm not.'

'As sure as God made little apples and the state of Texas, those are two men in grey suits and if you assure me they are carrying hardware then, ma'am, I will certainly believe you.'

He watched with Jill as the boat passed under the forty-fifty bridge, the forty-seventh and the forty-ninth. Two men stood on each, and the order of rotation was clear.

'There's six of the guys, all right.'

'That's what I thought.'

'And you on your honeymoon? The bastards. Pardon me, ma'am.'

'That's all right. Many of my best friends are . . . never mind.'

Her limited contact with Americans showed that the harder you joked, the less they laughed, and the more serious they became. In any case, Spencer Tracy was now in full, indignant flow.

'The low-down, cheapskate, commie bastards.'

'Commie?'

It was like the eleven-plus entrance examinations of long ago, where you had to pick the odd one out in a list of words like: sheep, cow, pig, escalator, goat.

'I think I should tell you, many of my best friends are . . .'

164

He did not allow her to finish the sentence.

'Don't worry. I am giving this whole matter my immediate and total attention. The United States will not be undermined by a gang of schmuks like those guys. Pardon me, ma'am, if you're Jewish.'

'No, I'm not Jewish.'

She wondered whether she should mention several of her best friends, but decided it would be pointless. Her self-appointed protector was gazing at some personal horizon, probably with a startling resemblance to the Alamo. Any minute she expected him to produce a bugle and summon the cavalry or at least lead the passengers on the boat in two choruses of 'The Battle Hymn of the Republic'.

'Stay close to me, ma'am, and the US of A will guarantee your security. Stay close when we disembark. Tell your husband.'

She shook Trevor once, twice, and at the third shake he stirred, opened his eyes, and said, 'Where am I?'

'Rotterdam.'

'Has it been raining?'

She spoke quietly but urgently into the most convenient ear.

'Listen, Trevor. There are six men watching us. The men in grey suits. You know the ones?'

'You mean . . . the men in grey suits?'

'There! Look!'

The boat passed under the fifty-third bridge. The men were there, in their duly appointed place, governed by whatever laws of the universe controlled their actions.

'Go home you bums!' Trevor shouted. Then he giggled: 'I'm feeling better.'

'Shutup and listen. When we get off the boat, stay close to him.'

She pointed to the American.

'Who is he?'

'An American friend.'

'Didn't know you knew any Americans.'

Trevor's numbed lack of comprehension made Jill wonder whether she had made a mistake in shackling their destiny to the stars and stripes.

'Ah, your husband's awake,' said the American.

'Well, he does impressions,' said Jill.

'Pardon me?'

'He looks just like Spencer Tracy,' said Trevor.

'You think I look like Spencer Tracy? You would not believe how many people have said that. My dear departed wife, God rest her soul, always said I should enter for one of those look-alike competitions.'

Trevor lowered his voice so that the Tracy look-alike would be unable to hear.

'Why do we have to stay close to him?'

'I think he's planning a rescue operation.'

'Are we sinking?'

'From the grey men!'

Spencer Tracy was having whispered conversations of his own with two or three members of his party. Then he turned to Trevor and Jill.

'Do you guys have any luggage?'

'Hey, that's really interesting,' said Trevor, wide awake suddenly. 'You call people guys, whether they're men or women and where I come from we call people men, whether they're men or women.'

'Yes, we have luggage,' said Jill, ignoring Trevor's semantic ramblings.

'Where is it?'

'At the place we bought the cruise tickets. You see, we haven't checked in at our hotel yet. But that's all to do with

Mr Veeler and wandalism and I'd rather not complicate your life any further.'

'OK, guys, here's what you do.'

For one terrible moment, Jill thought he was going to say, let's do the show right here and now. Instead, with equal urgency, he gave his suggestions though they came out more like orders. He was MacArthur, Eisenhower, Patton, seasoned with just a pinch of Fort Baxter. If they made it back to base, Jill felt, there was every chance of a crap game or an all-night session of stud poker.

'When we get back to the landing stage, go to the ticket office and grab your bags and baggage.'

'We could grab our coats and grab our hats and leave our worries on the doorstep,' suggested Trevor, with the born-again brightness of a man who had survived the worst hangover in world history and was rediscovering the simple joys of speech, movement and breathing. Spencer Tracy and Jill ignored him. They were good judges. The boat was passing beneath the sixty-seventh bridge and the grey men were looming overhead.

'I'll stay close by you,' Tracy continued, 'and so will my good buddies here.'

Jill and Trevor looked across the centre aisle of the boat and checked out the good buddies; they looked like older versions of Jack Benny, Harry S. Truman and Leo Gorcey, one-time leader of the Bowery Boys.

Spencer Tracy continued his briefing.

'We're travelling by coach. It's blue in colour and its number is 556. We are the European Tour of the Ancient Order of Elks, from San Diego in California. All of this is clearly written on the side of the coach in bold script. Our courier is male, Caucasian, six feet tall, weighs in at around two hundred pounds I would guess, and he carries a yellow parasol. But don't let that fool you. He's a pretty mean courier. If we lose you and if you lose us, watch out for that yellow parasol. You got that?'

'Yeah, I got that,' said Jill, entering into the spirit of the occasion.

'I'll follow you,' said Trevor, still confused by the patterns of sobriety. In many ways, drunk was easier.

'We'll murder the bums,' said Leo Gorcey.

'We owe them one for Pearl Harbour,' said Harry S. Truman.

'I'm thinking,' said Jack Benny.

The operation was somewhat anti-climactic, though Gorcey and Co. were clearly spoiling for a fight. The good buddies stayed close to Jill and Trevor as they recovered their luggage from the ticket office, then pushed their way quickly through the crowds of tourists on the quayside to coach number 556. They were waved on board by the courier with the yellow parasol, who seemed unconcerned that two English teachers had infiltrated the ranks of his ageing Elks.

Jill and Trevor sat near the back of the bus, with Spencer Tracy and Jack Benny in front of them, Truman and Gorcey behind.

'I told you we'd murder the bums,' said Gorcey.

'It makes you feel a whole lot warmer inside, on account of Pearl Harbour,' added Truman.

Jill, despite her gratitude, felt obliged to challenge this sentiment.

'Those men are not Japanese,' she said.

'So what? Nobody screws the US of A, whoever they are. They do so at their peril.'

'And we're English,' Jill persisted. 'These men, who are not Japanese, are following us, and we're English.'

'Lady,' said Truman, 'two hundred years ago, my ancestors

168

came to America from the village of Cheltenham in your beautiful state of Gloucestershire. For that, I owe you.'

He pronounced the name of the ancient county with at least seven syllables. It was impressive. Jill, unable to cope with an argument that linked eighteenth-century Cheltenham with Pearl Harbour, sat back in her seat and gazed out of the window. She thought she glimpsed two grey-suited men on a street corner but the coach accelerated and the men were out of sight.

Trevor wondered whether any of the Americans were jazz fans, or perhaps even jazz musicians; but after his experiences with Sam Bentley he was resolved to proceed with caution, until he was quite sure that he was better.

Jill found herself thinking about D. H. Lawrence. It happens to most literate people at intervals and some of them never truly recover. She pondered a phrase Lawrence used about the narrow-minded bigots who banned his books, and subjected him to fifty-seven varieties of persecution. He called such people the Grey Guardians. It helped her to come to terms with her predicament; she was being pursued by the Grey Guardians. It was good to be in the company of Bert Lawrence, despite their obvious ideological differences.

Trevor, having dismissed thoughts of jazz from his mind, temporarily, looked out of the window. The coach had left the centre of Rotterdam and was speeding along a motorway, except it was probably called something else. Was it autobahn? Autostrada? He saw a road sign, and nudged Jill from her Lawrentian dreams.

'We just passed a road sign. It said Airport in about four languages so it must be true.'

'Airport?'

'Whenever they give things subtitles, it proves they're serious.'

Jill leaned forward in her seat and tapped Spencer Tracy on the shoulder.

'Excuse me, I wonder, could you answer a question?'

'My pleasure, ma'am.'

'We've just passed a road sign saying Airport.'

'That's good news, ma'am, because that's exactly where we're heading.'

'I see.'

'And then the wagons will roll, we'll get the show on the road and before you can say Edgar J. Hoover we'll be in Athens.'

Jill sat back in her seat.

'They're going to Athens.'

'That's good,' said Trevor, 'I've never been to Athens. I've heard it's very nice.'

'But we're supposed to be looking for the school trip.'

'I never wanted to go on the school trip.'

Jill looked at him with a quality in her eyes that was no more than a cough and a spit from true love.

'Trevor, you are wonderful.'

'Isn't that what I keep telling you?'

She slipped her hand under his arm. 'You're very bad at underpants and socks but give you a major crisis, and you just shrug your shoulders and say, yes, that'll be all right, pet.'

'A jazz fan stays cool, baby, under all difficulties.'

The coach slowed down a little as it hit heavy traffic near the airport approaches. It was in a long stream of cars. Some of them may have contained Grey Guardians, maintaining surveillance on Trevor Chaplin and Jill Swinburne, but they, for a while anyway, were strictly on the sunny side of the street.

'We'll go to the Acropolis,' said Jill.

'Great,' said Trevor. 'I haven't been to the pictures for ages.'

Ten

Absorbing two itinerant teachers from the outer limits of Leeds into a party of tourists from San Diego in Southern California was less of a logistical problem than it appeared at first glance. The Americans had left town a week earlier, forty strong, on their European tour. Leo Gorcey explained what had happened next.

'So we stop some place. We stop in Paris. We stop in Brussels. What happens? One or two of the guys go walk-about, they find some action, it's time to hit the road, they don't show. What we gonna do about it? There ain't a one of us under seventy years of age. A guy finds some action, that's a bonus, right? He winds up dead, so he dies with a smile on his face. He winds up in prison, so we send in the marines. Myself, personally, I don't see no problem.'

The courier with the yellow parasol saw no problem either. 'I count them off the bus. I count them back again. As long as it adds up to forty, who am I to object to a few strange faces? I left San Diego with forty persons. I shall return with forty persons. If they are the wrong persons that is no longer my problem. I shall be on the next flight out with another forty persons. I rely on the self-balancing tendencies inherent in the human condition.'

The yellow parasol man, a graduate in creative jargon, had ambitions to be a White House press officer and spent hours in front of the mirror, burnishing his blandness.

By the time they were on the plane, flying to Athens, Trevor had spoken to most of the Californian Elks. He was disappointed to discover that not one of them was a jazz fan. Leo Gorcey was a good old country music freak, and produced a large hat by way of evidence; Harry S. Truman liked middle-of-the-road standards – the good old ones – and if provoked would slacken his tie and sing that he'd left his heart in San Francisco; Spencer Tracy had a large collection of Dire Straits albums at home; while Jack Benny had been listening to music all his life, without arriving at any firm conclusions. He was still thinking about it.

'Does it occur to you,' Jill said to Trevor, as she looked out of the window at clouds, 'that this is totally ludicrous?'

'No,' said Trevor, 'it's only a bit ludicrous.'

'Let's consider the situation.'

'All right.'

'We can go to Athens with these Elks. That is perfectly simple. We're travelling on their tickets and apparently we can stay in their hotel at their expense.'

'It's a very good arrangement.'

'But what do we have in our pockets? We have return tickets to and from Rotterdam. I suppose what I'm really saying is how the hell do we get home from Athens?'

Trevor gave this dilemma serious consideration for three and a half seconds. 'We watch out for some Elks from Leeds. Or Bradford. Or Wakefield.'

She gave him the look that meant: this is not a time to jest and dally. 'I want a serious answer, Trevor.'

'OK. Serious answer. I don't know. Therefore we have two choices. We worry about it. Or we do *not* worry about it. It's no contest.'

Jill had heard it all before: the Trevor Chaplin cure-all approach. It was the advice he would have given to the captain of the Titanic after it had struck the iceberg, to

Robinson Crusoe after he found the footprint, to Adam and
Eve after they tasted the fruit: 'You have two choices. You
worry about it. Or you do not worry about it.'

It was an attitude that Jill admired in some ways, but she
could not identify with it. She wanted to change the world.
Trevor wanted to leave it alone, on the understanding that
the deal was mutual and the world would leave him alone.

Nor could Jill decide whether this fundamental difference
made them incompatible in the long term. Was their relationship ultimately doomed? Or ultimately secure? Was it true
that people operated like magnets; like poles repelled and
unlike poles attracted?

Jill tended to worry about these things. Trevor did not.

Good Californian Elks only stay at the best hotels. Trevor
and Jill found themselves staying on the Syntagma, the main
square in Athens, adjacent to the Parliament building. The
hotel had five stars, was recommended by everybody from
Michelin to the MCC without asterisks or footnotes, and the
Americans insisted Trevor and Jill should have the honeymoon suite. It had been booked as part of the package as a
practical joke on the oldest Elk, but he had disappeared in
Paris, last seen in Montmartre with a pair of apache dancers.

The bedroom had a canopied double bed the size of a
decent smallholding, flowers on the table and complimentary
champagne in an ice bucket. Trevor picked up the telephone.

'What are you doing?' said Jill.

'Ringing room service. I'll ask them to send up a duvet.'

'Put that phone down.'

He put the phone down and wandered into the bathroom.
Jill heard raucous laughter, of the sort he generally reserved
for the wit and wisdom of Bobby Thompson, the great ethnic
comedian from Tyneside.

'Whyebuggerman!'

It was a coded message meaning: come and look at this, Mrs Swinburne. Jill went into the bathroom. It was a temple to the science of plumbing and the arts of cute vulgarity. The bath was hexagonal with golden taps, the wc and the bidet were similarly gilded and sat, one beside the other, apparently waiting for a brace of Royals keen to take part in an original variant on a Coronation ceremony. The enclosing walls had been built without a single right angle, and they were all mirrored, as was the ceiling.

'I've counted,' said Trevor. 'When I'm having a pee, I'll be able to see myself from thirty-six different angles.'

'You shouldn't look. You should close your eyes.'

'If I close my eyes, I might miss.'

'You couldn't miss a thing that size, even with your eyes closed.'

It was a prodigious display of everything Jill hated: materialism gone mad, conspicuous consumption, a reckless waste of raw materials and human ingenuity in a world where millions were starving and without shelter. And she adored it.

'Get out,' she said, 'I'm going to have a long, hot soak.'

'There's room for two in that bath,' said Trevor. 'I've paced it out.'

'We haven't come all the way to Athens, the cradle of civilization, for sexual perversion. We can get all that in Yorkshire.'

They bathed, separately and independently. Trevor shaved. They unpacked their case and he watched, in admiration, as Jill hung his shirts on hangers and placed them carefully in the built-in wardrobe. She treated clothes with the respect he gave to his Duke Ellington records.

He rang room service, having promised not to mention duvets, and ordered sandwiches and coffee. When they

174

arrived, Trevor realized he had no Greek currency to tip the waiter, a beautiful young Athenian god. He gave him the choice: Dutch guilders, British sterling or a credit card. The waiter opted for guilders and Jill made a note: she would write to the Chancellor of the Exchequer, telling him of the pound's status around the Aegean, when she returned home. She amended her mental note: *if* she returned home.

With their coffee and sandwiches they drank the champagne. Not to do so would have been an insult to San Diegan hospitality. It was a hot day and the sun shafted through the windows, highlighting the room's vulgarity.

'Here's to us?' said Trevor, raising his champagne glass.

'I'll drink to that,' said Jill.

She looked across at the bed, then at her companion.

'Howay the lads?' she murmured softly.

Cleopatra could not have made a more luscious approach. As often happened, Trevor made her giggle at a crucial stage in their mutual passion by asking a question: 'What do you do with a bidet?'

She started laughing, then said, 'Now look what's happened!'

'You told me I mustn't look.'

They both laughed, and they passed the afternoon in good, uninhibited, semi-tropical pursuits, without a thought for classical antiquities or what was showing at the Acropolis.

'It's called siesta,' said Jill as they travelled downstairs in the mirror-lined, high-speed, gilded lift.

'You mean everybody goes to bed in the afternoon?'

'Yes. But usually they get up before half-past six.'

The Californian Elks were gathered in the lobby. Most of them had passed their siesta in the hotel bar, apparently on the basis that they could sleep on their return to San Diego.

Leo Gorcey spotted Trevor and Jill as they tried to leave the building undetected.

'You two guys coming downtown with us? We're figuring on finding a piece of action. You fancy cutting yourself in, grab a slice, you're welcome.'

Trevor figured he had already sliced as much action as the human system could absorb during the last forty-eight hours. Jill galloped to the rescue.

'We're planning to stroll up the Acropolis, see the Parthenon. Then we'll stroll across to the Agora. Then maybe we'll stroll into the Plaka later in the evening.'

'That's a whole gang of strolling you got there, lady,' said Leo.

Trevor echoed the thought as they left the hotel, untrammelled by Elks.

'That sounded like a whole gang of strolling,' he said.

'The proper way to see Athens is on foot. In addition, the taxi drivers are on strike.'

During one of their spasms of afterglow – or half-time, as Trevor liked to call it – Jill had heard shouts coming from the square. She had looked out of the window to see a huge demonstration taking place in the Syntagma. The banners were hand-painted in exotic Greek letters and Jill had no idea of the cause that united the marchers: it could have been Elks Go Home, Zorba For Pope or Why Not On Sunday? She rang the hotel desk and was told: the taxi drivers are on strike.

They strolled up the Acropolis to see the Parthenon. Jill's attention alternated between a study of the buildings and a study of her guidebook.

'This is the Parthenon,' she said.

'Great,' said Trevor.

They strolled around the Parthenon, unique among the

thousands of tourists there present. They were the only people not taking photographs of each other.

'And this is the Erechtheion with its famous Caryatid porch.'

'Great. What's a Caryatid?'

'The beautiful stone maidens holding up the roof are called Caryatids.'

'Bet their heads hurt.'

They strolled down the gentle slope towards the main entrance of the Acropolis. Typically, they had come in the back way and planned to leave by the front door.

'And this is the Propylaea.'

'Great. It's easily the best Propylaea I've ever seen.'

'Trevor.'

He braced himself; he knew he had been asking for trouble.

'I bring you to the world's greatest architectural monument. This is where civilization was invented. It's where democracy was invented. And all I get is a string of cheap one-liners. Bet their heads hurt and easily the best Propylaea I've ever seen.'

Trevor put on his best show of earnestness and recited the speech he had been rehearsing during their long and mostly uphill stroll, knowing it would be needed.

'I'm sorry, pet,' he said, 'but you bring me to places like this, and it is amazing, and it is great, really, it is. Bloody great. But you can't expect a man who spends his life surrounded by wood shavings and sawdust to say anything more than that. It's great. Message ends.'

What he thought was: every time I look at one of her temples or caryatids, if I look slightly to the left or to the right I see two men in grey suits looking at us, and she'd see them as well, if she wasn't looking at the guidebook all the time, to tell me what I'm supposed to be looking at.

For once, Jill did not read his thoughts. She accepted his

spoken message at its face value and was grateful for it. When he wore his spaniel face, he was usually sincere.

He was breathing hard by the time they reached the Agora.

'Let's buy a newspaper when we see one,' he said.

'What is it you want? Not football results, surely.'

'See if the taxi drivers are going back. I'm knackered with all this strolling.'

'It's good for your metabolism.'

'I'd forgotten about metabolism.'

They walked the bounds of the ancient market and civic centre, where once Socrates had walked and where, at the appointed time, he had stood trial and tasted the hemlock. They felt closer to Socrates than to adrenalin and fibre, nuclear waste and Peterson, Mr Wheeler and the school trip.

Jill pointed her guidebook at a trim, octagonal building in marble.

'The Tower of the Winds.'

'What does it do?'

'It measures the wind.'

'You can't measure wind. It goes on for miles in every direction.'

'It measures the direction, you lunkhead.'

Trevor pondered the concept.

'I don't know, though. They were clever lads, these Athenians. I think maybe they could have measured the wind, if they set their minds to it.'

Then, as Jill leafed through her guidebook, Trevor saw them again: two Grey Guardians, standing in the shadows of a Doric temple at the top of a green hill. He realized that the real world was upon them: a world of men who watched and listened, bugged and reported, to protect shabby ideas that Socrates would have spat out before breakfast. Grey Guardians were not interested in measuring the wind; they would rather lock it up in a cell.

'Let's stroll a bit further,' said Trevor, abruptly, and for the first time that day, he chose their direction.

It was all the fault of Melina Mercouri.

She was one of Jill's heroines, along with selected members of the Pankhurst family, Winnie Mandela, and Sylvia from the Old Folks Home. Melina Mercouri had made the leap from actress to politician, at the same time that Greece had made the leap from military dictatorship to democracy. She was fighting a tough battle for the recovery of the Elgin marbles from whoever it was that nicked them and, according to an article Jill had read in a colour supplement, she had restored the Plaka to its original homespun glory.

Ms Mercouri had taken the Plaka, the ancient heart of the city, nestling in the shadow of the Acropolis, and cleansed it of all tackiness. She had persuaded the pimps and con-men, the porn merchants and the money-lenders to move on to some other temple, and she had a good line in scourging. If the colour supplement was to be believed, she had restored the Plaka unto the people and Jill loved her for it.

And it came to pass that Jill took Trevor by the hand and led him down the meandering streets, paraphrasing Chandler as they strolled: 'Down these meandering streets my man must go, my man who is not himself meandering.'

Trevor had no idea what she was talking and said so.

'It would take too long to explain. Like ten or fifteen years.'

Instead she gave him a quick rundown on key words likely to be useful in enjoying the full fruits of the area in a generally unconfused way. Bouzouki was music and you listened to it, souvlaki was food and you ate it, retsina was booze and you drank it.

'Retsina. That sounds great. Is it made out of cricket bats?'

'The Greeks don't play cricket. That's why they're always laughing. I believe Socrates examined cricket and found it lacking in beauty and logic.'

'In that case, can I have some retsina please, miss? My head's properly better now and my system's thoroughly cleaned out.'

They found a restaurant in a small square, at the intersection of two meandering streets. The tables were canopied by trees. The waiters shouted a great deal but with good humour. From several directions at once came assorted versions of the theme music from 'Never On Sunday'. A woman came to their table selling flowers. A man came to the table selling pistachio nuts. They bought three weeks' supply of flowers and pistachio nuts. Mangy cats hung around, like serfs at the lord's table in the great castle. Jill told Trevor not to give any food to the cats, so he threw them a flower, and then poured a glass of water over them. Had he behaved like this in a restaurant in the outer limits of Leeds, he would have been asked to leave. In the Plaka he was more likely to be given a drink on the house.

Jill Swinburne and Trevor Chaplin ate, drank and were merry in traditional Athenian style and his credit card was welcome. It was a wonderful meal and a wonderful evening and it was all the fault of Melina Mercouri.

When it was finished they stood at the intersection of the meandering streets.

'Now,' said Jill, 'we must think very hard and very carefully and try to remember where we live.'

'I should have brought the van. I've got a compass in the van.'

But Trevor's van was a continent away.

'Let's try logic,' said Jill.

'It'll never catch on.'

'Think about it. We have a choice of four streets, and it must be one of them.'

'Find the right one and we've cracked it. I mean, what do you think of that one? It seems a canny enough street to me.'

They looked along the street that Trevor had chosen. At the far end, where the lights from the cafés and shops dimmed away to darkness, stood two men, two Grey Guardians.

The merriness sank like a stone.

'Do you see what I see?' asked Jill.

'Yes,' said Trevor, 'and I'll tell you something else for nothing. That is definitely not the way home. I think that's the way home.'

He turned on his heel, a full hundred-and-eighty degrees and looked along the street that ran opposite. At the end of that street, too, were two Grey Guardians, standing where the lights had gone out as shops and cafés had closed. It was as if the Plaka were closing down for the night in concentric circles, gradually focusing on the little square where Trevor and Jill were marooned. Soon it would be a tiny pool of light in a hostile darkness stretching towards infinity, in every direction.

They checked the flanking streets. At the end of each of those stood two men.

'That proves one thing,' said Trevor.

'What?'

'Four streets. Two men in each. That means there's more than six of the buggers.'

'But which way home do we go?'

'Like the man said, I'm thinking.'

Trevor thought. Jill thought, too. They thought very hard indeed. Between them, their best offer was a question from Jill.

'What we gonna do now, Butch?'

It was a stock line they used in moments of crisis.

'Well, it was easier for Butch Cassidy and the Sundance Kid. They only had five mysterious horsemen chasing them.'

'Seven,' said Jill.

'I thought it was five.'

'I'm sure it was seven.'

They stopped abruptly, realizing simultaneously that they were in great danger, and arguing about how many mysterious horsemen there were, even in a very good movie, was not the most helpful of ploys.

'I have a suggestion to make,' said Trevor.

'What?'

'If we wait here, they come for us, that's eight of them and two of us. If we head up one of the streets, any one of the streets, that's two on to two. It's better odds.'

'We're not going to fight them.'

'We can't keep running away, Jill.'

She would never forget that moment. It was the first time she could remember his calling her Jill. There had been no shortage of homely Geordie endearments and often he called her Mrs Swinburne or miss, in imitation of the kids in school, but he had never called her by her first name. Not only that, he had done it in the context of a lousy B picture line.

'We can't keep running away?' she echoed.

'I just said that.'

'It's a dumb thing to say.'

'It's true.'

She had to agree. It was true.

'OK Butch, let's go meet them.'

They selected a street totally at random and walked along it, out of the bright lights of the square, and into the shadows. The men waited for them, not moving. Their faces were in shadow. Jill and Trevor came closer, their footsteps clattering on the cobbled surface. Jill wished she had worn shoes that were more casual, quieter. Trevor remembered clattering into the hall in his funeral shoes and wondered whether he would ever see Mr Wheeler again.

They approached the two men, who stood close together in the centre of the street. It made sense to walk either side of them and this they did, only to find their arms seized, calmly, efficiently and savagely.

'You must come with us and answer questions.'

In the darkness it was impossible to tell which of the men had spoken.

'You have no right to do this. I'm a British citizen,' said Jill, wishing she could think of a better reason.

'You must come with us and answer questions.'

'Gerroff!'

Trevor tried to free himself from the man's grip. He wondered whether it was worth trying the black belt ploy. No, he decided.

'You must come with us and answer questions.'

It was like a looped tape fed into their grey skulls. Jill tried Plan B, which had served her well on previous though less dramatic occasions. She screamed. Her grey man clamped his hand over her mouth. She bit it.

Then, above the screams and shouts and the repeated phrase about answering questions, a stentorian voice echoed across the length and breadth of the Plaka.

'Why, it's average-sized Mrs Swinburne! And her friend and ours, Mr Chaplin! This is nice!'

Up the steps from a basement club climbed Big Al, mastermind of the white economy in the outer limits of Leeds, highly regarded stand-up philosopher and staunch ally of Jill and Trevor in their previous year's adventure that had sent two eminent but corrupt citizens to jail and a senior police officer into premature retirement.

He was followed up the stairs by his brother, Little Norm. Al was fond of introducing his intimates to strangers with the

183

words: 'I'm Big Al, that is Little Norm and this is average-sized Mrs Swinburne.'

Big Al and Little Norm were followed from the club by a gang of sturdy artisans from the outer limits. Jill realized it was one of Al's redundancy trips. Part of his white empire was devoted to promoting cheap holidays for workers recently made redundant, thus disposing of the redundancy payments quickly and with good humour, and making the beneficiaries qualify more speedily for the State's charity.

This particular party, it emerged later, was from a steel rolling mill, closed in the cause of greater efficiency and a leaner, fitter national economy. The men were not lean. In many cases, their beer bellies preceded them up the stairs by several minutes. But they were strong, decisive, Yorkshire and willing.

Big Al, who matched his name and had once seriously contemplated setting up in business as a freelance Pennine, had assessed the situation quickly. His valued friends, Mrs Swinburne and Mr Chaplin, were being forcibly apprehended by two total strangers in a foreign country. It was a situation up with which he would not put, and neither would his comrades from the rolling mill, enlivened as they were by large helpings of bouzouki and retsina.

It was an old-fashioned fist fight. Big Al hardly participated. He acted as a benign chairman, overseeing the contest, ensuring fair play, providing the right team won. Even when the two grey men were joined by six additional grey men, it simply added spice, without tilting the balance.

It was an easy victory for the away team. The final score was Grey Guardians 0, Big Al's Rolling Mill All-Stars 8.

When it was over, Big Al shook hands with Jill and Trevor. 'It's been a great pleasure to meet the two of you again. How have you been keeping? Are you still listening to your funny music, Mr Chaplin? We've got some nice records at the warehouse if you're interested. . . .'

He seemed unconcerned about the fight. Jill had to interrupt: 'Before you set Trevor off on the subject of jazz . . . thank you for coming to the rescue.'

Big Al smiled. 'Just a little fracas in the Plaka.'

Eleven

The man from the Embassy was a little brusque.

He arrived at the hotel as Jill and Trevor were having an early breakfast, just before noon. A few tattered Elks were also in the dining room, discussing their various nights before.

'You find any action?' asked Leo Gorcey, of nobody in particular. His eyes had retreated far inside his head and he did not expect normal vision to be restored until late in the afternoon.

'Me, I found myself a great heap of *son et lumière* by the Parthenon,' reported Spencer Tracy.

'They'll give you a shot of something at the hospital,' said Harry S. Truman.

Jack Benny was staring at the menu, trying to decide what flavour of Alka Seltzer would speak most eloquently to his condition.

'And what about you guys?' said Leo, seeing two shapes nearby that vaguely related to his memory of their English companions. 'You find any action?'

'Yes,' said Trevor, 'we got ourselves into a street brawl in the Plaka. Twenty, maybe thirty guys. We left eight of them more or less unconscious on the sidewalk, then moseyed on down here before the cops showed.'

'Trevor . . .'

Jill reprimanded him, with a discreet, low murmur, and a sharp, under-the-table kick.

'You're putting me on,' said Leo. 'It's that goddamn English sense of humour, it slays me. A street brawl? You hear that, you guys? These guys claim they were in a street brawl, you guys.'

'Which guys?' asked Spencer Tracy.

While Leo Gorcey was clarifying the guys issue to Spencer Tracy, there was an announcement on the hotel PA system: would Mr Chaplin and Mrs Swinburne please go at once to the reception desk. At the desk they found the man from the Embassy and he was a little brusque. He took them quietly to one side. He spent a large part of his working life taking people quietly to one side. In his considered view, they were more likely to respond to his words if they were taken quietly to one side first.

'It is my considered view,' he said to Jill and Trevor, once he had taken them to one side, 'that last night's incident in the Plaka was, to say the least, unfortunate. That is our considered view at the Embassy.'

He had not referred to the nature of the incident; he assumed that they knew what he was talking about. Jill had taken an instant dislike to his public school/Oxbridge tie, manner and lower lip, and decided to make him work harder.

'Incident? What incident?'

'Come, come, Mrs Swinburne, you must be aware of the incident I am talking about.'

'You mean the punch-up?' said Trevor.

'The incident,' repeated the Embassy man.

'He means the punch-up,' said Jill.

He was shuffling now. The smooth exterior and crystalline vowel sounds concealed a bear of very little brain. He tried to regain the initiative.

'It is our considered view that it would be in the best interests of the UK if you left Athens as soon as possible.'

'You want us to get out of town?' said Jill.

187

'That is our considered view.'

He recited a brief catalogue of cut-price phrases from the handbook he had been given on his first day: acute government embarrassment, national security, sensitive relationships, the world role of the UK, strength of sterling, inflationary tendencies, infiltration by militants. The more he said, the less he belonged to any real world that Jill or Trevor inhabited. Once again she dragged him back to earth.

'Let me get this clear,' she said. 'It is your considered view that in the interests of world peace, or words to that effect, we should get the hell out as soon as possible?'

'I would hesitate before agreeing to your precise diagnosis, but yes.'

'Well, it won't be easy, since we are in Athens, and all we have is what we stand up in.'

'Plus a bloody big suitcase,' added Trevor, 'and the return halves of two tickets from Hull to Rotterdam.'

'You might be able to persuade North Sea Ferries to make a détour by way of Piraeus, but it'll screw up their timetables,' said Jill, warming to the task of needling the upper crust. The man from the Embassy became very brusque.

'We'll fly you back to London!' he snapped.

'Yeadon,' said Trevor.

'Yeadon? What is Yeadon?'

'We live in the moonstruck outer limits of Leeds,' Jill explained. 'London is a long way away.'

'Mind you,' said Trevor, 'we could check who's playing at Ronnie's . . .'

'Yeadon!' Jill repeated.

The man from the Embassy sighed, hesitated, wondered about reconsidering his considered view, then nodded.

'We'll fly you back to . . . Yeadon.' He obviously visualized Yeadon as the last place in England where sabre-toothed tigers still prowled, sniffing the air for human flesh.

'First class,' Jill threw in, to top up the deal.

There was another pause, as the parties to the dispute viewed each other across a huge chasm, divided by diction, cadence, parentage and a thousand nuances as old as time.

'Club class,' said the man from the Embassy.

It was his final offer. Jill and Trevor accepted it, firmly, politely, but without handshakes. He promised the flight tickets would arrive within the hour, by special messenger. They watched him walk across the lobby and out through the swing doors. They hoped he would trip but his sort rarely did.

'Heigh ho and lackaday,' said Jill. 'I shall miss the Californian Elks.'

'They're just like Three B,' said Trevor, 'but sixty years older. That's my considered view.'

They arrived home on Friday. They had left on the Monday. They had been pursued across seas and across continents. They had been too preoccupied to send postcards, and had spent too much time indoors to get much of a tan.

Nothing had changed. The *Guardian* reported a cabinet split, a rained-off Test Match and street violence in Athens, said to have been caused by soccer hooligans. They assumed this was the considered view of the press attaché at the Embassy.

There was a small heap of mail: three bills, five advertising offers, a friendly computerized letter from Readers Digest and a postcard from Sylvia.

Sylvia's card showed a smiling portrait of Mao Tse Tung and on the back was written: 'The ducks are hungry. Bring bread. Down with imperialist hyenas. Love. Sylvia.'

'What does that mean?' asked Trevor.

'It means she wants to go in the park to feed the ducks.'

The pattern was refreshingly domestic and normal. Peterson did not hang around the street corner, and Grey Guardians had seemingly disappeared from the face of the earth. Trevor wondered whether it was their Wakes Week.

There was one moment of high drama when Trevor thought his van had been stolen, but Jill reminded him that it was parked on the dockside in Hull. They planned a trip for the following Sunday. They would go to Hull by train and return with the van.

They sat in the living room and made other plans.

'You can choose,' said Jill. 'Either you go to the shop for some milk, or you can unpack the suitcase.'

'Does unpacking include hanging neatly in wardrobes and folding neatly in drawers?'

'Naturally.'

'I'll get the milk.'

Trevor stood up, and crossed to the door. Jill stood up and crossed to the foot of the stairs. It was inevitable they should meet in the hallway.

'Tell you what,' said Trevor. 'This is really ordinary.'

'The school trip's due back on Monday. I should think Mr Wheeler will want a brief word, don't you?'

'Like . . . you're sacked?'

'Very like that, I should think.'

'No sweat,' said Trevor. 'We'll open a health food shop.'

On Saturday morning, Jill took Sylvia to the park. She forgot to take any bread because Trevor had forgotten to bring any from the shop. He pretended that he had examined the bread on offer, but found it wanting: all white and chemical, he said, but truth was he had forgotten.

The ducks looked fatter than ever and the two women

were not concerned about their welfare. Nor was Sylvia impressed with the tape that Jill had left with her.

'No disrespect, comrade, but I checked your tape from top to bottom, and it's a load of bollocks.'

'Seriously?'

'Seriously. Genuine, guaranteed, high pedigree, twenty-four carat bollocks.'

An ultra-sensitive listening device poised high over the outer limits on that Saturday morning might have picked up an interesting related pattern of sounds: Sylvia's first 'bollocks' coincided to the split second with the doorbell ringing at Jill's house, and her repetition of the word coincided, as precisely, with the moment that Trevor opened the door.

He wore his Saturday morning uniform of an old gabardine raincoat, now serving as a dressing gown, on top of his pyjamas. He had promised Jill he would get up as soon as she left the house but had gone back to sleep. The doorbell had woken him up, or at least dragged him one-third of the way to consciousness. The person on the doorstep dragged him the other two-thirds.

'Sergeant Hobson!'

'No longer sergeant, Mr Chaplin, but still Hobson!' his visitor responded smartly, with a click of the heels carrying more than a hint of self-satisfaction.

'You'd better come in,' said Trevor, not out of politeness but because it was a chilly morning and though it was summer, in a technical sense, there seemed to be a touch of frost on the unfrocked bank manager's wishing well.

Hobson walked into the living room and sat down. A year earlier, as a keen-eyed graduate copper, he had masterminded the investigation that had sent his own commanding officer into oblivion and he knew his own strength. In a period of weeks he had transformed himself from village idiot to conquering hero and pulling a stroke like that gave a chap confidence.

'No Mrs Swinburne?' he asked, looking around the room.

'In the park, feeding the ducks.'

'I see.'

He did not see, nor did he believe, but that was the Hobson style.

'What I have to say concerns her as much as you, Mr Chaplin. May I wait?'

Trevor shrugged, meaning: yes, you might as well, it's Saturday morning and I'd rather read the sports page and play a little jazz but it's down to you, sunbeam.

'Thank you,' said Hobson. He cast an investigative eye around the room. 'Have you been putting up more shelves, Mr Chaplin?'

'Yes. They knocked my house down so I moved in. Me and Mrs Swinburne, we're cohabiting. In sin. All good stuff. I do the washing up. Also we have a lot of fibre and metabolism.'

'I see.'

Hobson did not see. Like Mr Carter, he found most conversation from the Swinburne/Chaplin axis tricky to cope with. It was like trying to nail down globules of mercury.

'I'd offer you some coffee but we've only got instant and we never drink instant. Not now. I've transformed my consciousness. Doesn't half make your eyes water.'

'I see.'

Sylvia explained the course of her investigations as Jill wheeled her around the park. It was too cold to sit beside the lake. The ducks had been stamping their feet to keep warm.

'I listened to the tape. It sounded exactly as you said. Men

192

in a room, talking about dumping nuclear waste in one of the Dales. But somehow it didn't sound real. I've been listening to fascists all my life. All shapes, all sizes, all colours, all languages. These were not real fascists. It was almost like a game.'

'A game?'

Sylvia nodded.

'I consulted a comrade. He's a sound engineer with one of the major national broadcasting organizations. Those people who present a middle-of-the-road, balanced view of the world, in accordance with the wishes of the government of the day. My comrade played the tape. He said it was phoney. He said it had been recorded over a period of time and edited afterwards. He also said it sounded like the men were reading from a script.'

'You don't have scripts for confidential meetings about nuclear waste.'

'You can hear paper rustling on the tape.'

'I heard the paper rustling,' said Jill, 'but there's always lots of paper at meetings. Minutes and balance sheets and feasibility studies and sub-committee reports and garbage like that. . . .'

'Not garbage like that, Jill, garbage like a written script. My sound engineer comrade said the paper rustling comes at regular intervals, as if they're turning the pages of a script. My comrade knows. He's worked on radio plays. It's his nightmare, actors who can't turn a page without making a noise. In addition to actors with belly-rumbles and rattling false teeth.'

Jill pushed the wheelchair past the swings and concealed fish pond where she and Trevor had first encountered Dave the wimp. It seemed a generation ago. Had they been intimidated by Peterson, pursued by Grey Guardians and thrown out of Athens all because of a fake? It made no sense.

Then she remembered the words of John the barman, after he had risen from the dead: 'In a crazy world, the biggest idiot is bound to be king.'

Hobson was helping Trevor to dry the dishes when she returned to the house.

The two men had sat for an hour, waiting for her. They had run out of conversation after ten minutes. Trevor played him some Bix Beiderbecke – 'for old times' sake' he had said, but Hobson remained baffled – and offered him the morning paper. Hobson had browsed through the *Guardian* warily keeping its rampant radicalism at arms' length.

He greeted Jill with relief. He found Trevor extremely hard work.

'Sergeant Hobson!' she said.

'No longer sergeant, Mrs Swinburne, but still Hobson!' he repeated, along with the heel click.

Jill was surprised how pleased she was to see him again. She had always regarded him as a grey-suited man, but felt there was a streak of colour interwoven somewhere, striving for release; not a primary colour, to be sure, but a pastel shade, pleasing to the senses.

Dishes washed, dried and impeccably filed away, Trevor, Jill and Hobson sat down in the executive living area with their coffee. Trevor had relaxed his principles and made instant, though he scowled his disapproval as he drank.

'That's awful.'

'You're getting to be a bore, Trevor. Now. Sit quietly and listen to what the nice policeman has to say.'

'Not sergeant, not even a policeman,' smiled Hobson. Whatever it was he was, he was proud of it. Jill had a very good idea what it was.

'Don't tell me,' she said, 'you're now MI something. MI13 or MI17 or MI23. I bet it's an odd number.'

'You obviously wouldn't expect me to tell you everything, but in principle you are quite correct. And it *is* an odd number.'

'I knew it would be an odd number.'

'Same as the bridges in Rotterdam,' said Trevor, maintaining his record of never saying anything that Hobson could understand. Jill, for her part, decided to maintain her record of never losing the initiative in a conversation with Hobson.

'And I expect you've come here to talk about tapes?'

'Yes,' agreed Hobson, 'partly about tapes.'

'Highly confidential tapes that could be damaging to the nation's security if their contents were exposed to the public gaze?'

'That . . . kind of thing, yes.'

'And no doubt you have reason to believe that I came into possession of such a tape and want to know what I did with it?'

'Yes.'

'It's in a safe place,' said Trevor.

Jill stood up, put down her empty coffee cup and walked across the room to Hobson. Suddenly she had energy to spare and a spot of pacing became necessary.

'Let me tell you this, Mr Hobson. We have been harried by people like you, asking about that tape. The house has been searched, from top to bottom, twice to my certain knowledge. At all times, I have denied knowledge of such a tape.'

'But that was a lie, Mrs Swinburne.'

'Of course it was a lie!'

'Thank you, Mrs Swinburne.' He smiled again, pleased with himself for having extracted the truth about the lie.

'But I will tell you something else, Mr Hobson,' she

continued, building up a good head of righteous indignation. 'That tape was a lie, too. That tape was a pack of lies, from start to finish.'

'Ah.' The Hobson smile faded.

'Game, set and match, Mr Hobson?'

She sat down.

'Mrs Swinburne . . .' Hobson began.

'I'm here too,' said Trevor. 'I got chased across Europe as well.'

'Mr Chaplin, Mrs Swinburne,' Hobson began again, praying Jill would not challenge him on the issue of addressing the man first: 'I think we owe you an explanation. Have either of you heard of . . . disinformation?'

'Disinformation?' said Jill.

'I've heard of disinfectant,' said Trevor, then added, as he saw Jill looking at him, 'shuttup Trevor.'

'I know about disinformation,' said Jill. 'It's a process of feeding lies into the system, hoping they become truth. The South Africans are very keen on it. Somebody in darkest Shropshire writes a letter to the *Daily Telegraph* saying that when he was in South Africa he saw black people dancing in the streets of the townships out of sheer joy at the good times they're having under apartheid. The letter goes in the paper. And with a bit of pushing and shoving it becomes the truth. The black people of South Africa dance with joy all the time. Isn't that how it works?'

'That's . . . the principle of the thing,' said Hobson.

'Are you in charge of disinformation, Mr Hobson?' Jill asked.

'It comes within my orbit.'

'I always wanted an orbit when I was a lad,' said Trevor, 'but my dad was out of work. Be quiet, Trevor.'

'Perhaps you'll allow me to explain what happened with the tape,' said Hobson.

'No,' said Jill, firmly, 'I'll tell you what happened to your tape. A bunch of amateurs in your department put that tape together and allowed it to pass into the hands of a bunch of amateurs on *our* side.'

Hobson checked in his notebook. 'The PLFWY?'

'The PLFWY,' agreed Jill. 'I'm not sure why you passed it on to them. Yes I am. You expected them to use it in their tatty community newspaper. Then somebody picks it up on the radio or television and you, or somebody like you, issues an official statement saying it's a lunatic invention of subversive elements. Which, for all practical purposes, it is.'

'There are still twenty-three things I don't understand, Inspector,' said Trevor.

'Trevor!'

'I'm serious!' Trevor insisted. He stood up. 'I think I'll walk about for a bit.'

He paced up and down, the length of his record shelves, like an unarmed guard protecting his heritage as, at most times, he was.

'The tape's full of crap. So why bother trying to frighten us?'

'To maintain the illusion that it was truth. If we behave as if it's true, that reinforces your belief that it is true.'

'That's what bothered me,' said Trevor. 'If you'd really wanted it back, your people would have really broken our bones. You'd have beaten the shit out of us till we owned up.'

'Precisely. Not me personally, you understand.'

'We understand,' said Jill.

'Another department,' said Hobson.

'And would I be right in thinking,' said Jill, 'that there were several agencies pursuing us and frightening us? Peterson was one lot, the grey men were another lot?'

'Absolutely,' Hobson replied, proud of Jill's confirmation

of the infinite number and variety of the security services. 'When the nation's security is threatened, the security services must leap into action, and what's more, they must be *seen* to leap into action.'

He beamed at them, a man halfway up a beguiling career ladder, doing well, unconcerned with what lay at the top: a bigger, smarter, nastier man waiting to stamp on his fingers.

'One more question,' said Trevor.

'And then you must bring in your surprise witness,' said Jill.

'Shuttup Jill.'

Trevor's reaction startled all three of them.

'Ask your one more question, Mr Chaplin, and then I really must go. I'm already late for my next assignation.'

'If your tape . . . your disinformation . . . your pack of lies about the dumping of nuclear waste . . . if you're spreading that around to fool idiots like us . . . does that mean somewhere there's a true story? Real plans to dump real nuclear waste in a real place?'

'Obviously nuclear waste has to be dumped somewhere. It follows there are plans to do so. It follows that all such plans are highly confidential.'

'Thank you. No more questions.'

Trevor sat down. Jill, who had remained silent and thoughtful through his unexpectedly passionate cross-examination, took his hand, then looked hard and sadly at Hobson.

'What's a nice young man like you doing in a cesspit of a career like that?'

'I have to confess, Mrs Swinburne, the answer is . . . rising.'

Twelve

It was the worst of terms, it was the worst of terms.

The staff and students of San Quentin High were in no doubt about the autumn term. An entire academic year stretched ahead of them, a long bleak road with no turning and no perceptible destination. Exhortations to GCE and CSE students to work hard now and not leave it until the night before the examinations in the following May were greeted, at best, with derision. The Job Centre raffle for this year's vacancy was always drawn at Christmas, and they would miss it anyway.

On the playing fields of San Quentin, the goalposts were put up, ready for the football season. They were taken down by vandals. They were re-erected. If they survived November the Fifth the school football team might complete its fixtures. PE teachers ran up and down the touchline screaming 'Keep it tight at the back!' and 'Chop him! He can't run without legs!', imbuing their young charges with the noble traditions that had won the World Cup for England in 1966.

In the staffroom, Mr Carter laughed unrelentingly about the school trip to Holland. As with Trevor and Jill's stay in Athens, the Embassy had intervened and sent the party home ahead of time, though not club class. Mr Wheeler had locked himself in his cabin – 'trying monasticism for size' according to Mr Carter – and charges were still pending as a result of the kids' activities. The Dutch and British governments were having top-level talks about extradition treaties, relating to Yvonne Fairweather's stay in Rotterdam.

The best thing about the autumn term was the weather: it was warmer than summer, and on several days the fog cleared and there was visibility the full width of the playground.

To their surprise, Jill and Trevor were not victimized by the headmaster for their failure to participate in the school trip. The first week of term passed by and he did not mention the subject, partly because he was still in deep shock. Then, at the beginning of the second week, they were summoned to his study. They passed through the buttons, bells and decompression chamber that protected him from Three B and original sin.

'Mr Chaplin, Mrs Swinburne, you may have been wondering why I have not, thus far, spoken to you about the school trip to Holland.'

'We guessed there was a good reason like, perhaps, you didn't want to talk about it,' said Trevor.

'The fact of the matter is, I *know* why you failed to arrive at school in time to catch the bus.'

'You know?' said Jill, mildly surprised that the headmaster knew anything.

Mr Wheeler glanced out of the window, a man now and forever haunted by shadows and shrill phantoms.

'Soon after our return I was visited by a mutual friend of ours.'

Jill and Trevor thought: this is ludicrous – none of our friends would touch Wheeler with a bargepole and he has no friends.

'I promised him I would not reveal his identity to a soul, but if I tell you he is a graduate and was a police officer, you might guess . . .'

'Hobson,' Trevor broke in.

'I promised not to reveal . . .'

'Somebody bearing a remarkable resemblance to the former Sergeant Hobson,' Jill suggested, 'but not necessarily him?'

'Precisely, Mrs Swinburne. This person, whom we will not specify by name, assured me that you two spent the summer doing confidential work involving national security. Not just confidential work but highly dangerous work.'

'Well,' said Trevor, 'there was a bit of a fracas in the . . . .'

The headmaster held up a hand indicating: say no more.

'I simply want to assure you that the matter is closed, my lips are sealed and . . .' He hesitated, then continued: '. . . and I would like to thank you, on behalf of Great Britain.'

Trevor and Jill said thank you: it was the best they could manage, without laughing.

That evening it was Trevor's turn to make supper. They ate stuffed aubergines. Jill was unusually quiet.

'Something wrong with the meal?' said Trevor.

'No.'

'Good. 'Cos I tried really hard with it.'

'There's something I have to tell you, Trevor.'

'Go ahead. Talk it through.'

She pushed her plate to one side, then leaned forward, closer to him. 'You remember how we packed in a hurry the day we set off for Holland?'

Trevor nodded. He was still eating.

'And you remember the hot passionate siesta in Athens in the honeymoon suite?'

Trevor nodded. He was still eating.

'Well, in the hurry to pack I forgot my pills, and now it looks like I'm pregnant.'

Trevor stopped eating.

'Whyebuggerman!'

'Is that all you have to say?'

'No. It's funny that, you being pregnant. I was just thinking today we'd got the place looking really nice and maybe two people weren't quite enough. I was going to suggest getting a dog. I've always wanted a red setter. . . .'

'Trevor!'

It was sharply said, not angry, but firm.

'Shall I look into your eyes for a minute while I think of something sensitive?'

'I wish you would.'

They looked into each other's eyes, daring each other to break the silence. Jill spoke first.

'I want to have the baby. The only thing is . . . what sort of world is it to bring babies into? People telling lies about nuclear waste because the truth's even worse? Grey Guardians on every corner? Men who are proud of their violence?'

Trevor spoke second: 'I'm new to childbirth, pet, but I've watched other people. From a safe distance. It's the cleanest thing I know. So let's show the buggers. Let's do the cleanest thing.'

He put a hand on her shoulder.

'Eat your supper. I can't abide waste.'

ALAN PLATER

The Beiderbecke Affair

Trevor Chaplin, woodwork teacher and jazz freak, and Jill Swinburne, English teacher and Conservation candidate in a Council by-election, form the most reluctant detective partnership in the annals of investigation. Their precinct lies in the moonstruck outer limits of uptown Leeds.

A beautiful platinum blonde offers Trevor a set of rare Bix Beiderbecke records at cut rates and thereby Chaplin and Swinburne are drawn into the ferocious crossfire between local government corruption and white marketeers. They walk mean streets inhabited by Big Al, Little Norm, Harry the Supergrass and his dog Jason, and the ubiquitous McAllister brothers, while the zealous Sergeant Hobson, BA, maintains learned surveillance on every corner.

The Beiderbecke Affair is Chandler with flat vowels, Hammett with dropped aitches, McBain with mushy peas and extra chips.

DAVID NOBBS

Second from Last
in the Sack Race

Growing up in the thirties and forties, a podgy school-
boy who is no good at games and not exactly brilliant
at work, Henry Pratt faces many problems. War,
peace, mothers, fathers, aunts, uncles, boys, girls,
God, conscience, toilets both inside and outside,
sexuality both latent and blatant, all these provide
difficulties for him. His name makes people laugh,
and his accent is mocked by Southerners. His life becomes a search for a means of survival. But Henry is
a fighter, and he develops a survival technique which
is intriguing, and utterly convincing.

'Indefatigable gentleness and joyous delight . . . shine
through a bruising black comedy which will make you
laugh out loud.'

Gay Firth, *The Times*

'His eye for the nuances of a Yorkshire childhood of
the thirties is superb.'

Yorkshire Post

'Clever, deftly written and wonderfully funny.'
Nicholas Best, *Financial Times*

Top Fiction from Methuen Paperbacks

While every effort is made to keep prices low, it is sometimes necessary to increase prices at short notice. Methuen Paperbacks reserves the right to show new retail prices on covers which may differ from those previously advertised in the text or elsewhere.

The prices shown below were correct at the time of going to press.

☐	413 55810 X	**Lords of the Earth**	Patrick Anderson	£2.95
☐	417 02530 0	**Little Big Man**	Thomas Berger	£2.50
☐	417 04830 0	**Life at the Top**	John Braine	£1.95
☐	413 57370 2	**The Two of Us**	John Braine	£1.95
☐	417 02100 3	**Waiting for Sheila**	John Braine	£1.95
☐	417 05360 6	**The Good Earth**	Pearl S Buck	£1.95
☐	417 05810 1	**Man of Nazareth**	Anthony Burgess	£1.50
☐	413 57930 1	**Here Today**	Zoë Fairbairns	£1.95
☐	413 58680 4	**Dominator**	James Follett	£2.50
☐	417 03890 9	**The Rich and the Beautiful**	Ruth Harris	£1.75
☐	417 04590 5	**Sometimes a Great Notion**	Ken Kesey	£2.95
☐	413 55620 4	**Second from Last in the Sack Race**	David Nobbs	£2.50
☐	413 52370 5	**Titus Groan**	Mervyn Peake	£2.50
☐	413 52350 0	**Gormenghast**	Mervyn Peake	£2.50
☐	413 52360 8	**Titus Alone**	Mervyn Peake	£1.95
☐	417 05390 8	**Lust for Life**	Irving Stone	£1.95
☐	413 53790 0	**The Secret Diary of Adrian Mole Aged 13¾**	Sue Townsend	£1.95
☐	413 58810 6	**The Growing Pains of Adrian Mole**	Sue Townsend	£1.95
☐	413 58060 1	**The Set-Up**	Vladimir Volkoff	£2.50
☐	413 55570 4	**Charlie**	Nigel Williams	£1.95

All these books are available at your bookshop or newsagent, or can be ordered direct from the publisher. Just tick the titles you want and fill in the form below.

Methuen Paperbacks, Cash Sales Department,
PO Box 11, Falmouth,
Cornwall TR10 109EN.

Please send cheque or postal order, no currency, for purchase price quoted and allow the following for postage and packing:

UK	55p for the first book, 22p for the second book and 14p for each additional book ordered to a maximum charge of £1.75.
BFPO and Eire	55p for the first book, 22p for the second book and 14p for each next seven books, thereafter 8p per book.
Overseas Customers	£1.00 for the first book plus 25p per copy for each additional book.

NAME (Block Letters) ....

ADDRESS..

....